"Heather, call me as soon as you get this!"

Zach yelled, as if she might hear him despite talking into her voice mail. "Lock the doors. Make sure the alarm is set. I'll be there in–" he glanced at the clock out of habit "–five minutes."

Zach ended the call and pressed the accelerator to the floor. In the not-so-far distance behind him, he could hear sirens. He hoped they were racing to the Lapp home and not to pull him over for driving like a lunatic.

Up ahead, smoke filled the air in a thick black plume, disappearing into the dark storm clouds. His heart plummeted.

His truck skidded on the wet pavement as he slowed at Heather's driveway. He slammed the gear into Park and jumped out of the truck, leaving the door open and the engine running.

He ran as fast as he could toward the barn. "Heather! Heather!" Zach screamed, then he hooked his arm over his mouth and pushed into the smoky confines of the fire.

Dear Lord, let her be okay, he prayed.

Alison Stone lives with her husband of more than twenty years and their four children in Western New York. Besides writing, Alison keeps busy volunteering at her children's schools, driving her girls to dance and watching her boys race motocross. Alison loves to hear from her readers at Alison@AlisonStone.com. For more information, please visit her website, alisonstone.com. She's also chatty on Twitter, @alison_stone. Find her on Facebook at Facebook.com/alisonstoneauthor.

Books by Alison Stone

Love Inspired Suspense

PLAIN SANCTUARY

ALISON STONE

H HARLEQUIN LOVE INSPIRED® SUSPENSE

Recycling programs
for this product may
not exist in your area.

LOVE INSPIRED BOOKS

ISBN-13: 978-0-373-67811-2

Plain Sanctuary

www.Harlequin.com

Printed in U.S.A.

Give all your worries and cares to God,
for He cares about you.
—1 Peter 5:7

To Scott, with love, forever and always

ONE

"Walker." Deputy U.S. Marshal Zachary Walker answered his cell phone and held it in front of him set on speakerphone. He dropped his duffel bag on the floor of his rarely used hunting cabin. He hadn't had a chance to open the windows to air out the place before the call came in. It was probably just as well considering the rain pelting the sides of his family's cabin.

"Hi, Zach." It was his boss, Dave Kenner, at the U.S. Marshals Service at the Western District of New York headquarters in Buffalo. And if his boss was calling him late on a Friday night at the start of what was to be Zach's vacation—a vacation his boss had to force him to take—he knew it wasn't to make small talk. "Are you in Quail Hollow yet?" Zach pulled out a chair at the kitchen table and waited for his boss to get to the point.

"Yeah, just got here." He cleared his throat.

"Remember that vacation you told me I had to take?"

"You never thought you'd have a nine-to-five job as a U.S. Marshal, did you?" Dave exhaled sharply over the line. Something was seriously wrong. "You see the news?"

"No." Zach had left the office at six, stopped to visit a college friend and his family for a few hours, then listened to an audiobook on the hour drive to Quail Hollow. It was his attempt to decompress. Transition. Leave the stress of the job behind. So, no, he hadn't listened to the news.

"Let me bring you up to speed."

"Am I no longer on vacation?"

"That remains to be seen."

"Hold on." Zach stood, set his phone on the counter, grabbed the remote and aimed it at the nine-inch TV sitting on the kitchen counter. The laugh track of some sitcom filled the quiet room. He immediately hit the down arrow on the volume and then played with the bunny ears mounted on the TV. He refused to pay for cable at his getaway cabin.

"Let me fill you in."

"I had no doubt you would." Zach didn't try to hide his frustration. He had worked for Dave long enough to know when he was avoiding getting to the point. That could mean only one thing: the news had to strike a personal chord.

Zach flipped the channels blindly, sensing his blood pressure spiking.

"It's Brian Fox."

And there it was.

A headache exploded behind his eyes. He dragged a hand over his mouth. Just then he clicked on a channel and a live news broadcast appeared on the screen. Searchlights lit the stone walls of Peters Correctional Facility like a scene out of some prison break movie. A woman with a blond bob and a red coat stood with a mike in one hand, pressing the other to her ear, waiting for directions from her producer or whoever called the shots at the studio in a situation like this. The words on the bottom of the screen scrolled past. Zach had to squint to read them as the reception cut in and out to the old-school TV: "Convicted murderer Brian Fox escaped Peters Correctional Facility at 8:15 p.m."

He swallowed hard as disbelief made the words flicker even more.

Over two hours ago.

Zach muttered under his breath. "You gotta be kidding me. He escaped? How in the…?" He rubbed his temples with his fingers. The image of his little sister, bloodied and sprawled on his back steps with a trail of blood leaking from her head, flashed in his mind. Bile rose in his throat. People had told him he'd have closure when Fox was convicted. Put behind bars. The people who'd claimed that had never experienced the brutal death of a loved one. Peace. Closure. They were elusive.

"How did this happen, Dave?"

"Initial speculation is that he had help from the inside."

"Help?" Zach paced the small space. "Who helps a convicted killer escape?" He closed his eyes against the flickering image on the TV, feeling a migraine coming on.

"A female employee may have provided him tools. She's missing now, too. He's resourceful. Fox dug a hole through the cement wall in his cell. Got into the bowels of the prison, then, it appears, he got out through the sewer system."

Zach fisted his hand. "You're kidding me. He was able to do this without anyone noticing?"

"Apparently he knows how to turn on the charm. Had this woman wrapped around his finger…" His boss's words trailed off when he realized he had opened mouth, inserted foot. Fox had turned on the charm with Zach's sister. Married her. Then showed his true self when it was too late. "I'm sorry. I know this is personal for you."

Zach ignored the last comment. That was the only way he got through each day. The only way he was able to do his job. Each day he did his best to catch the bad guys, something he did in memory of his little sister. But he had yet to find a way to do his job and not be haunted by the horrific scene in which she died.

He was successful in shutting down the dark thoughts maybe 20 percent of the time, at most. Despite helping other people, he'd never get past failing the one person who had spent her entire life looking up to him.

I'm sorry, Jill.

"Brian Fox's on the run." His boss got back to the facts.

"Any idea where he's headed?"

"His first wife moved to Quail Hollow about nine months ago. She's renovating an old house. Word is she's opening a bed-and-breakfast."

"She's here in Quail Hollow?" Dread pooled in the pit of his stomach. This wasn't the first time Zach had wondered how a guy like Fox landed not one, but two wives. "Does Fox know where she is?"

"Not sure. But his cellmate said he's fixated on her. Blamed her for putting him in prison."

"Great. The jerk kills my sister and he blames his first wife for his imprisonment. What a delusional idiot."

"About that vacation…" his boss said, a hint of hesitancy in his voice.

"I'm officially off vacation."

"I need you to track down his ex-wife. Put her in protective custody until we have Fox back behind bars."

"Give me her info."

Dave rattled off an address for the woman. "Listen, we couldn't find a phone number, but we found her current address from a public real estate transaction. Fox could do the same thing."

"Well—" Zach sighed "—Heather Miller hid for ten years from this guy. She only came out of hiding to testify against him in my sister's murder case. I owe her."

"Keep your head on straight. If it gets too personal, I'll send someone else in."

Zach gritted his teeth. "I'm already here."

"I know. That's why I called. Besides, they have every law enforcement agency in Western New York tracking Fox. I can't spare another person. Stay cool. And I'll let you know as soon as we have him in custody. It shouldn't be long. And let me know when you make contact with Miss Miller."

"Will do." He ended the call and grabbed the car keys from the table. So much for rest and relaxation.

* * *

A crack of lightning illuminated the night sky in the distance. The stillness felt electric. A sense of expectation hung in the air. Swallowing around a knot of emotion, Heather Miller adjusted the plain roller shade on the bedroom window. A light breeze blew in from the cracked window and with it a mist of rain and the scent of country air.

Her *mammy* had lived out her life in this home, looking out this same window at the barn and the seasons that cycled through tall rows of corn and barren land. How had her *mammy* been able to look at that barn every morning and night? The dilapidated structure hunkered in the shadows, a silent reminder of a tragic event that had changed the course of all their lives. Back then, could her *mammy*, Mariam Lapp, ever have predicted that her descendants would be living as outsiders, defying their Amish roots?

Heather had been six years old when her father slipped out of town with his three young daughters in their long dresses and bonnets. That was the last time she had seen this house, her *mammy* and her Amish wardrobe. Their father had stopped at a superstore outside of town and purchased his daughters cheap sneakers and *Englisch* clothes and they'd never looked back.

The memories of that day were both disjointed and etched in her memory. The bright white sneakers. Her first pair of jeans. The colorful unicorn on her T-shirt.

Her heartbroken father had taken what was left of his family and carved a life for them in the outside world. Leaving the Amish was one of a handful of events that had shaped Heather into the woman she was today.

Today was yet another milestone. A happy one.

Heather was back in Quail Hollow, an *Englischer*, planning to run a bed-and-breakfast for all the tourists interested in seeing the Amish countryside. The inheritance had come as a surprise and Heather hoped her grandmother wouldn't mind that her eldest granddaughter had opened her home to the outside world in this way.

Heather was excited by the possibilities. She had come a long way since she had fallen for a charmer when she was only nineteen. Now she was making a second—no, a third—go at life in a place that held her roots, yet she'd never felt more free.

She would learn to live in the moment and let go of the past.

Moving away from the window, Heather flipped back the covers and climbed into bed.

She pulled up the hand-stitched quilt passed down to her through generations. She was exhausted but feared she wouldn't sleep. Without a TV or Wi-Fi, her options for wasting time were limited to reading and her eyes were too tired for that. Besides, she needed to try to rest. She had another long day ahead of her. The house still needed work before opening weekend in a couple weeks. Just in time for the peak autumn colors. She had hoped to remain in her nearby apartment until renovations were completed, but time and money had run out.

Just as she settled her head on the pillow, a thunderclap made her jump and the resulting rumble vibrated through the walls of her new home. A whoosh of wind rustled the oak tree on her front lawn. A vague memory whispered across her brain. Had her father brought her back here to play on a tire swing hanging from its limbs? Or was that a memory from before their family moved out of the home they shared with their *mammy*? Her mother had been an only child, a rarity in the Amish community, and she and her husband had moved into the home with Mariam to start their family. When Heather's mother died and her father left Quail Hollow, her *mammy* had been left alone in this big house.

Heather closed her eyes and imagined the

wind blowing through her long flowing hair—free from the constraints of a tight Amish bun—as she pumped her legs on the swing. Despite the vivid memory, or maybe it was a dream, her father claimed he had never gone back to Quail Hollow. He couldn't face the tragic past. Heather forgave her father that. His wife—Heather's *mem*—had been murdered by a stranger passing through town, or so they suspected. No one was ever arrested. Every corner, every face, every waking moment in Quail Hollow had reminded him of all he had lost.

All *they* had lost.

Heather threw back the quilt, climbed out of the bed and was drawn again to the window. Thick drops of rain pelted the glass and screen. She pushed down on the frame and it slid with a loud screech, making the hairs on her arms stand on edge. A shadow in the distance, near the rows of corn, caught her attention. She blinked rapidly. It was gone.

Am I imagining things?

Heart racing in her chest, she flattened herself against the wall, careful to stay out of view.

An old, familiar fear coiled around her lungs, making it difficult to breathe.

Heather focused on each intake and release of breath as the walls seemed to close in around her.

In through the nose, count to three, out through the mouth…

In through the nose, count to three, out through the mouth…

She was safe. The man who had tormented her was in prison. A hint of guilt twined with her fear and pressed heavily on her lungs. Somehow in her warped perspective, she felt guilty that after she escaped her violent marriage, he had sought out another victim.

His new wife hadn't been able to get away.

Brian Fox killed his second wife, landing him in prison. Finally granting Heather her freedom.

She closed her eyes and said a quick prayer for Jill's soul, the only remedy that gave her some modicum of peace.

Heather opened her eyes and focused on her reality. She was standing against the wall, still afraid of the bogeyman from her past. Perhaps she wouldn't have been so jumpy if the Amish workmen had completed the installation of the new window in the breakfast area. Large plastic tarps stapled over the huge opening may keep the rain out, but not a determined intruder.

She rolled back her shoulders, trying to dismiss her racing thoughts. She blamed Brian Fox for the lingering fear, the paranoia that always hovered just below the surface. A person didn't live in constant fear for ten years and not escape unscarred.

The wind picked up and the tree branches scraped the side of her home. She climbed back into bed and shuddered against the chill despite having closed the window. She'd have to hire someone to trim the branches. The dragging sound was unsettling.

Heather finally drifted to sleep when a loud crash downstairs startled her awake. She bolted upright in bed, her heart jackhammering in her chest.

"It's just the storm," she muttered to herself. "It's just the storm."

A creaking sounded in the hallway. On instinct, she slipped out from under the warm quilt and grabbed her cell phone from the nightstand. She moved to the bedroom door, considered locking herself in, or perhaps dragging the tall chest of drawers in front of it. Indecision kept her rooted in place. Why had she thought it was a good idea to move way out into the country all by herself?

In spite of her past fears, Heather decided she'd live life as a strong, independent woman, not letting her ex take that away from her, too. However, in reality, she was defenseless out here. Even if the spotty cell phone reception allowed her to call 9-1-1, how long would it take for help to arrive? Could law enforcement reach her before a potential intruder did?

Grabbing the golf club she always kept in the bedroom closet—this new home was no exception—she tucked her cell phone under her arm and opened the bedroom door. The loud creak of the hinges set her nerves on edge.

Since her grandmother had been Amish and she meant to recreate an Amish-like experience for the tourists, there was no light switch close by. Instead she'd have to take the time to turn the knob on the kerosene lamps mounted on the walls in the hallway.

An unease threaded its way up her spine as she tiptoed down the hallway toward the stairs. She grabbed her cell phone out from under her arm and used the back of her hand to feel along the wall in the dark. The other hand was wrapped firmly around the handle of her driver.

Dear Lord, please keep me safe.

Heather navigated the stairs, each one creaking under her weight. Breathing heavily, she made her way to the new addition off the kitchen, where she hoped to serve meals to large groups of tourists staying in her home.

The plastic sheets the Amish workmen had hung over the opening for the window flapped in the wind. The snapping sound—along with the rumble of thunder in the distance—was disconcerting in the dark of night.

For a long moment, Heather stared at the rippling plastic, trying to decide if she should barricade herself in the bathroom and call 9-1-1 because someone had slipped in through the opening or if perhaps the wind had somehow torn the plastic sheeting from its staples.

With her back flat against the wall, she didn't let go of the golf club. Her eyes adjusted to the shadows. A crack of lightning illuminated the new breakfast nook. A metal mop and broom had been upended and had come to rest in the corner.

A shaky groan of relief ripped from her throat as the need to both laugh and cry at the same time overwhelmed her. The metal bucket must have made the crashing sound. Not an intruder. She set the golf club against the wall, then examined the plastic sheet more closely. She couldn't leave it like that or the rain would warp the plywood that formed the base of the new hardwood floors that were scheduled to go in soon.

She glanced at the time on her cell phone. The workmen wouldn't be there till morning. And she couldn't very well call her Amish handyman this late at night. Even though he was allowed to have a cell phone for work purposes, she doubted he kept it on his bedside table as she had. The rules provided limits.

Come on, you can do it, a little voice inside her head nudged her. *You want to own a business? You gotta get your hands dirty. Put on your big girl britches.*

Rolling her shoulders, she tried to ease out the kinks. She might as well replace the torn plastic and seal the window opening because the adrenaline surging through her veins wasn't going to allow her to catch a wink of sleep anyway.

She turned on a kerosene lamp in the sitting room, then jogged up the stairs to throw on some clothes. On the way back down the stairs, she could hear the rain pelting the roof.

"Being a business owner is highly overrated," she muttered.

She grabbed an umbrella from the front hall, then put it back. She'd need two hands to carry the supplies from the shed in the back corner of the yard. She had noticed her Amish handyman, Sloppy Sam, putting them away this afternoon. The Amish people's tendency to use nicknames to distinguish between the same names was both creative and charming. She doubted she would have had a nickname because her name wasn't all that common among the Amish. Her mother's love for flowers influenced the names of her daughters: Heather, Lily and Rose. But the girls never had to worry about their unique names while living in Quail Hollow because they were ripped away from their extended family as little girls.

Focusing on the task at hand, Heather plucked her rain slicker from a hook by the door and stuffed her arms into the cold sleeves. She psyched herself up to run across the wet yard, get the stuff she needed from the shed and then return to the house. It would take no time. No time at all.

She laughed at herself.

She really was a chicken.

But she figured she came about it honestly, after being terrorized by her husband for years.

Brian Fox was in jail, she reminded herself.

And she was safe in Quail Hollow.

She unlocked the back door, a useless lock considering there was a large hole in the back wall of the house.

She darted back into the kitchen and grabbed a flashlight from the junk drawer and felt the weight of it in her hand.

What could happen to her in her own backyard?

Zach drove past the house with the address his supervisor had given him for Heather

Miller, made a U-turn about a mile up, then returned, pulling in alongside an Amish buggy that had been abandoned across the street and partially obscured his truck. Based on his limited interaction with Heather Miller during Fox's trial, he'd learned that she had gone off the grid for ten years, fearful for her life. But a year ago she resurfaced after Fox's arrest for murdering Zach's sister. Heather's testimony had been instrumental in putting him away for a long time.

For that, Zach was grateful.

Then, nine months ago, according to his boss, this real estate transaction in Quail Hollow popped up with her name on it. Poor woman probably let her guard down after Fox was arrested, figuring she'd be safe.

She should have been safe.

Drawing in a deep breath, he knew he had a job to do. He had to push aside his personal demons. His personal need for revenge. His job was to get Miss Miller into protective custody until Fox was back rotting in jail.

Zach killed the headlights on his truck, then studied the property, wondering why Fox's first wife had moved to a farm in Quail Hollow. From what he knew about her, she had grown up in Buffalo, New York. Not exactly the country. Maybe this was her way of starting over after Fox's imprisonment.

The reason why Heather Miller was out here in the middle of nowhere wasn't important right now. Securing her was.

Fox wasn't likely to announce himself, and the darkness didn't help. Zach thought he knew dark. But the blackness in the country during a rainstorm was unlike anything he had experienced. The wipers smearing the rain didn't help the cause.

He grabbed his cell phone from the middle console of his truck and called his boss. The call took a few extra minutes to connect. "I'm sitting outside Heather Miller's house. I'm going to check out the property before I try to make contact."

"Okay. Once you have her secure, report back in. And, Zach…be careful. Local law enforcement reported that Fox may have stolen guns from a home near the correctional facility. There was a break-in shortly after his escape."

Zach ended the call, then tucked the phone into the interior pocket of his jacket. He climbed out of the truck and closed the door with a quiet snick. The sound of thunder rumbled in the distance and the rain was still coming down steadily. The temperature had plummeted with the storm, not unusual in September in Western New York.

Maybe that meant Fox was hunkered down somewhere and not stalking his ex-wife.

As long as Fox wasn't hunkered down here.

Zach crossed the street, giving the house a wide berth, as if it might hold secrets. He noticed a light on in the kitchen that hadn't been on when he pulled up.

He scanned the landscape. There were a lot of outbuildings for a person to hide in. He was making his way around the back of the house when he heard a rustling at the back door. Sliding his gun from its holster, he rushed toward the door, focusing intently on the sound.

A person—a woman, based on her petite stature—stood on the porch with a flashlight. *What's she doing?* Before he had a chance to announce himself, she let out a scream that sent all his senses on high alert. The flashlight fell from her hands and landed with a thud on the porch. The light went dark. She spun around, pushed through the open door, then slammed it shut.

Zach froze in his tracks. He holstered his gun and lifted his hands in a nonthreatening gesture. He didn't want to frighten her any more than he already had.

"I'm calling the police," she yelled from inside the door. "Leave now!"

Zach reached into his coat pocket and pulled out his credentials. "I'm Deputy U.S. Marshal Zachary Walker. We met last year at Brian Fox's trial. I don't think my ID will fit under the door. Go to a window. I'll show you."

"Go away."

"Not gonna happen."

"Come back during the day. That's what a normal person would do."

"Ma'am, I wouldn't bother you so late at night if it wasn't important."

Silence stretched between them. He didn't hear any movements on the other side of the door, so he assumed she was still standing there debating what to do. After a moment, he heard rustling behind the door that sounded much like a dead bolt sliding out of place. The door opened a crack. A brass chain glinted when he lifted the flashlight she had dropped. A swift kick would have snapped the chain on the door, but he needed her cooperation, not her fear.

Heather squinted and lifted her hand to block the beam of light.

"Sorry," he muttered.

"Slip your ID between the crack. Hurry up." She spoke with an authority he hadn't anticipated.

Zach passed his ID through the narrow opening between the door and frame. She slammed the door shut. The dead bolt snapped back into place. After a long minute, he heard the slide of the chain and she opened the door.

Heather Miller planted a fist on her hip and a dark shadow crossed her face. "Marshal Walker. This can't be good."

"No. I'm sorry to have to tell you this. Brian Fox escaped and we fear he's coming for you."

TWO

Heather glared at the U.S. Marshal standing on her back porch in the middle of the night, his familiar face reminding her of how far she had come. His mere presence making her feel like everything she had worked so hard to build these past nine months was about to slip away.

No, no, Brian Fox was locked up in Peters Correctional Facility.

"May I come inside?" The deputy U.S. Marshal had a valid request. The small porch provided little protection from the weather. And the wind and rain pelting against the metal roof of the overhang was scraping across her every last nerve.

"Yes, of course." She would not allow herself to melt into a puddle of panic. She was not the woman she used to be. Despite her best efforts, her gaze drifted to the darkened yard beyond her porch and a chill crept up her spine.

"Come in, Deputy U.S. Marshal." She opened the door wider for him.

"Thanks, and please call me Zach." He slipped in past her, the rain from his coat dripping on the floor. He turned slowly to face her. In the yellow glow of the kitchen, she noticed the handsome angles of his face. The same intensity in his eyes from when she'd first met him at Brian's trial was still evident. Her ex-husband had murdered his little sister.

"How did Brian get out? I don't understand. He's in a maximum-security prison. You must be mistaken." Her mouth suddenly went dry and her knees threatened to give out from under her. She sensed she was standing on the edge, feeling like the unstable cliff she had built her new life upon was about to crumble beneath her.

"I understand he had help from the inside."

"No... How? I don't understand..." She shook her head slowly. The man who was standing in her kitchen grew blurry.

The marshal took a step toward her. "I know it's hard to comprehend, but we have reason to believe he's coming for you."

The man's words became jumbled and sounded like they were coming from the other end of a long, narrow empty tunnel. She blinked slowly, feeling as if she was floating above her body. Maybe if she pinched herself, she'd wake up from this nightmare.

Brian escaped. Brian escaped. Brian escaped.

Unable to wrap her mind around that simple concept. No, not a simple concept. A completely impossible concept. How did someone escape from a maximum-security facility? Even with help? She turned and placed the flat of her hand on the cool countertop, trying to ground herself. "Explain what's going on. *Now.*" Her fear came out as anger.

"Would you like to sit down?" He pulled out a chair at the small kitchen table, the one she'd sat at earlier planning the future of the bed-and-breakfast. Her future...

It took Heather a moment to hear his words, process their meaning. She looked up at him, trying to keep her lips from trembling. When had he moved to stand so close to her? Her anxiety spiked and she slid closer to the door. Away from him. Toward her escape.

Always have an escape.

That had been her mistake with Brian. She had been swept off her feet as a young girl. Married him. Then when things turned violent, she had no job. No place to run. No escape.

Until not escaping would have meant certain death.

It had for his second wife.

A shudder coursed through her and she wrapped her hands around the edge of the sink, ignoring the man's offer to sit down. Lifting her gaze to the window, she saw her hollow eyes reflecting back at her.

Was Brian out there watching her?

She spun around and squared off with the U.S. Marshal who had come to share this horrible news.

"What happens now? I'm renovating this bed-and-breakfast. I have plans…"

She looked up and tuned into the narrow wood shelf lining the top of her grandmother's plain pine cabinets. Her grandmother had a collection of hand-cut wood blocks that Heather recognized as buildings located in the center of Quail Hollow. She wondered if the Amish would have allowed such frivolous decorations, but Heather assumed her grandmother may have bent a few of the rules after losing so much. What punishment could the Amish elders have dished out to her *mammy* for a few wooden decorations when she had already suffered the worst fate: her daughter had been murdered and her son-in-law left Quail Hollow with her three young granddaughters never to return?

What would her *mammy* think if she knew

her granddaughter had almost suffered the same fate as her daughter? However, her mother had died at the hands of a stranger. Heather had been threatened by the man she had once loved. Were some families prone to violence?

Heather shook her head at the ridiculousness of that thought. Her mind had a tendency to race when she was stressed. To think the most random thoughts.

Focus.

Heather grabbed a glass from the cabinet and filled it with tap water. Then she turned to face the man in her kitchen. "Why do you think he's coming for me?"

But she knew, didn't she?

Her hand began to shake and she set the glass down. "I haven't had contact with him since… the trial." That was when she had finally faced the man who had abused her for years. When she finally stood up to him.

An emotion she couldn't name flitted in the depths of his eyes. "We have reason to believe he's obsessed with you and may be headed your way."

Thick emotion clogged her throat. "How is that possible?" But deep down she knew. Brian Fox was an egotistical psychopath and she had escaped his clutches. He'd also vowed that he would kill her if she ever left him. Her ex-husband didn't like to fail. Now he was taking his one shot at freedom to right his one failure.

Her.

Heather's entire body shook. The yellow light in the kitchen of the old farmhouse made her pallor more pronounced. She pulled out the chair and slumped into it, placing her elbows on the table and digging her fingers into her hair.

"Do you have someplace you can go?" Zach hovered over her, then realized he might get a better response if he sat down across from her. Less threatening.

After a moment, she glanced up. A silent tear slid down her cheek. Law enforcement officers learned to separate their feelings from the job, but this case was too personal not to feel heartache for this woman.

"No, I don't have someplace to go. I spent every dime I had on renovations. I moved out of my apartment today. *Today!* It's like he knew how to mess with me." She held up her palms, disbelief threading her tone. "I'm opening a bed-and-breakfast. I've decided to name it Quail Hollow Bed & Breakfast. Simple, but appropriate. Renovations are nearing completion. I've worked so hard." Her tone had a weary quality, probably a mix of her frustration with the contractors and the new bomb he had dropped on her: her violent ex-husband was tracking his way across Western New York to continue his reign of terror.

"Could you delay the opening? Just until Fox is back in custody?"

"Maybe he won't find me. It's not like I'm on social media or anything advertising where I live." The hope in her voice was like a knife twisting in his heart. How could one man cause so much havoc?

"We were able to track you down through a real estate transaction. Easily. He could do the same." Zach resisted the urge to reach out and cover her hand. Comfort her. But it wasn't his place. He hardly knew Heather. He only knew what she had done for his family. She stepped up at his sister's murder trial when it counted. Now he had to keep her safe.

Heather straightened and pounded a fist on the table. "That jerk took my twenties from me. I refuse to let him take any more."

Anger pulsed through his veins. "Fox could take your life."

Heather jerked her head back as if she had been slapped, but instead of crumbling, she seemed to grow angrier. She pushed back her chair. It slammed into the wall behind her, then crashed to the floor. She stepped over it and paced the small space. Then she turned to face him, jabbing her index finger in his direction. "Don't you think I know that? I left him in the middle of the night with only a few dollars and the clothes on my back. I made sure I stayed off the grid. I lost touch with my family. I moved every few months when I thought he might be closing in. I don't know when he stopped looking for me, but I know when I stopped fearing him. When he went to prison for murdering—" her voice faltered "—for killing your sister." She pressed her palms together and touched her lips with the tips of her fingers. "There's not a day that goes by that I don't pray for Jill. And there's not a day that goes by that I don't thank God for sparing my life."

Heather bent over and righted the chair and tucked it under the table. Wrapping her hands around the back of the chair, she leaned toward him. "I'm not going to run. I don't want to bring danger to anyone else's doorstep. I've run too often in the past to have established any solid friendships to impose upon. And I have no money to leave on my own." She placed her hand on her midsection. "It's like I'm trapped all over again."

"There have to be options. It shouldn't be long before they track Fox down. They have NYS Troopers, FBI Agents, and every other law enforcement agency between Quail Hollow and Peters Correctional Facility looking for him. They'll find him soon. But you must lie low for a few days."

A determined look settled in her eyes. "I've worked too hard. I refuse to let him control me again. The bed-and-breakfast is booked for opening weekend in a couple weeks. I have lots to do to get ready before then. If this place isn't ready and I cancel the reservations, I won't be able to pay my bills. I fear everything will spiral downward from there." She crossed her arms again and gritted her teeth. "I'm not going to live in fear anymore."

Zach stood to meet her frantic gaze. He knew this was anger and fear speaking. Not logic. "It's only temporary," he spoke softly.

She locked gazes with him. "I'm not leaving. I bet you can call your boss and convince him to have someone stay here to protect me."

He scrubbed a hand over his face, no longer bothering to hide his frustration. "My superiors are going to insist you go to a safe house."

"It's not going to happen. I'm staying here so I can continue getting this place ready and your office is going to see that I'm kept safe."

He cocked his eyebrow. "If I can't convince you to leave, how do you suppose I'm going to be able to convince my superiors to allow me to stay?"

"Because New York State won't like the bad press if they not only allowed a killer to escape from one of their *secure* correctional facilities, but in doing so, they let him get to one of his prior victims." Her tone was oddly cool, as if living in fear had made her numb. Or maybe she had reached the end of her rope and instead of letting go, she had decided to swing out with her legs and kick with all she had.

Heather held up the plastic sheet while Zach used the staple gun to secure the edges. She was glad she had something to occupy her hands, but she wished she could say the same thing about her mind.

Brian was out of prison and headed her way.

Her ex-husband had haunted the periphery of every part of her waking life and he had visited many of her nightmares.

But ever since he had been locked up in Peters Correctional Facility, she had allowed herself to hope, to dream, to make plans for a brighter future. Push him out of the center of her mind.

Tonight, Brian had come roaring back. The worst possible scenario was laid out before her. Despite her rioting emotions, she was not going to let him ruin this dream.

Erring on the side of caution, Zach had

searched her house for any intruders. Thankfully, everything other than the construction zone was secure.

"The workmen will be here in the morning, but if we'd allowed this rain to keep coming in, it would have ruined the plywood. I'd hate for the workmen to install the new hardwoods on top of warped subflooring," she said, feeling the awkwardness of the silence stretching between them.

"Yeah, no problem."

Cha-chink. Cha-chink. Cha-chink. Three more staples went through the thick plastic into the raw wood. Per Heather's instructions, Zach carefully aligned the staples so any holes they left would be hidden by the frame of the new window.

After they finished the task at hand, they sat in the rockers quietly, interrupted only by the occasional polite chitchat. Heather was unwilling to leave and Zach was unwilling to leave her alone. Heather's bones ached by the time the sun crept over the horizon. Finally she stood. "I'll make us some coffee." She started toward the kitchen when a knocking on the front door drew her attention. She glanced at the clock on the wall, surprised since it was so early.

"Hold up," Zach said, stretching out his hand to block her from going to the front door.

Heather did as he said, her heart in her throat. *Would Brian actually knock on the door?*

A soft voice floated in from the entryway. "Um, is Heather here?"

Ruthie! Heather rushed to the front door to find her Amish friend standing there with a basket full of fresh fruits and vegetables. "Hello, you're here early."

"I figured you'd be up, ready to start the day. If not, I figured I could let myself in and start without you."

Heather had forgotten she had given Ruthie a key.

"*Gut* morning." Ruthie cocked her bonneted head and gave Zach a pointed stare. "Have you hired extra help?"

"Um, no." It was too early to think on her feet.

Ruthie held up her basket of fresh foods. "I thought you might be low on groceries. Meanwhile, knowing what's in season, we can plan the menu for your first guests before the days get away from us. We have lots to do."

"Of course." Heather led the woman past Zach toward the kitchen. "It will be good to plan ahead." Get her mind off Brian.

As they passed near the new addition, Ruthie whispered, "You don't have to hide the fact that you hired workmen outside the Amish community."

Heather's lips formed into a perfect O, but she didn't know what to say. She didn't want to alarm her friend and employee. Nor did she want to offend her. Ruthie had recommended her good friend's work crew.

Guilt threaded through her. Was Heather placing others in jeopardy by not going into hiding? How long would it really take to capture a fugitive?

Heather racked her brain about how to best explain Zach's presence, when Zach approached and extended his hand, making the decision for her. "I'm Zach Walker, a friend of Heather's." Ruthie tipped her head in greeting but didn't take his hand. Zach smiled and dropped his hand. "I stopped by to see how the new construction was going." He pointed toward the window. "Good thing. The rain was pouring in the opening for the window."

"Another early riser?" Ruthie muttered, then turned her attention to the plastic covering the window. "I'm so sorry. Sloppy Sam should have had the window in already."

"I believe there was a delay by the manufacturer," Heather said, eager to ease Ruthie's concerns.

"I'm sorry for your inconvenience."

Heather waved her hand in dismissal. "It's fine. I suspect he'll have it in today. Then we'll have a beautiful new eating nook." She wandered over to the far corner of the window and inspected the staples. "I trust they'll be able to stain the woodwork the same color as the original wood throughout the house."

"My friend is *gut*. Just let him know, *yah*?" Ruthie nodded at Heather. "I'm going to take inventory of the canned goods in the pantry. I've been doing a little shopping since you hired me. We need to start planning our menu."

"Okay." Heather watched Ruthie walk away. She dragged her hand along the unfinished edge, marveling that yesterday her sole concern was getting the addition completed on time.

"Ruthie is going to help me with the day-to-day operations of the bed-and-breakfast."

Zach nodded his understanding.

Heather drew in a deep breath. She loved the smell of raw wood. She started to smooth her hand along the drywall when her eye caught something on the wall near the corner. In red permanent marker it read: Brian + Heather 4Ever.

Nausea swirled in her gut. She spun around, fear blurring her vision as she struggled to focus on Zach's face. "Brian. Brian Fox was here."

THREE

"I've already searched the house. He's not inside. Not anymore." Zach touched Heather's arm in what she assumed was intended as a comforting gesture, but how could she possibly be comforted?

Her ex-husband had been in her house. *He's here in Quail Hollow.*

Stars danced in her line of vision. Less than twelve hours ago this room had held so much promise for the future. For all the potential customers to her quaint bed-and-breakfast. Now its walls and the graffiti pulsed. A hot flush of dread crashed over her. She was suffocating. Trapped. She tugged on her collar and focused on her breathing.

"Are you *sure* he isn't still in here?" Her lower lip quivered. "Hiding." She found herself whispering to protect Ruthie from her past. Her chest grew tight at a memory of a confrontation with Brian. She had been out with friends.

Having fun. Something she hadn't done much since they got married. Brian hadn't let her. But she had been uncharacteristically defiant. Determined to reclaim some of her life.

A mistake.

Brian had been waiting. In the dark. Insanely jealous that she had been out with her friends. He had accused her of picking up guys. Something she would never do. She had grown to fear Brian, but she had never been unfaithful in her marriage.

That was the first time he had hit her. His fist had struck her, hard and fast, a shocking surprise in the darkness. She had been an easy target backlit by the hall light.

"Yes. I checked the house thoroughly." Zach interrupted her racing thoughts. "But we can't stay here. He's close."

"Who's close?" Ruthie asked, concern etched onto her pretty features, free of makeup, as she returned from the pantry on the other side of the kitchen. "Did someone break in?" She tugged nervously on the loose strings of her white bonnet.

Heather smiled tightly. "I'll explain in a minute."

Zach pulled back a corner of the vinyl sheeting covering the window. "What's in the building in back?"

"You saw the shed. It just has supplies for the remodel." She pointed to the stapler and vinyl. "The barn's empty. Needs some repairs." A thumping started in her head. "He's hiding in there, isn't he? He's in there." The hysteria welled in her chest, squeezing her lungs, making it difficult to breathe.

"Look at me," Zach said, a determined forcefulness in his tone. *"Look at me."*

She met his eyes and saw warmth, compassion and something she always saw in her own eyes when she looked in the mirror—anger. Anger aimed at a man who had ruined so many lives.

"I am not going to let anything happen to you. I promise."

Something about the sincerity in his voice, in his eyes, made her believe him. But hadn't she also believed her husband when he told her he'd never hit her again? That he was sorry.

She had been fooled by a charming liar.

But Zach wasn't Brian. Zach had come here to protect her. She had to trust him.

But trust didn't come easily.

He pulled back his jacket and she noticed his gun, immediately relieved that they weren't sitting ducks. He plucked his cell phone from his belt. "I'm going to call the local sheriff. Let them know Brian Fox may be close."

At the mention of his name a shudder raced through her. Apparently sensing her renewed dread, he reassured her that she'd be safe. "I need you and Ruthie to go to a room that locks. Your bedroom? A bathroom? And stay away from the windows."

Instinctively Heather reached out and grabbed his wrist. "No, wait for the sheriff before you go into the barn looking for him. Brian's evil."

Zach shook his head. "I need to go out there and check the buildings. I can't risk him getting away." He leveled his gaze at her. "You have a cell phone?"

She nodded, her palms growing slick as she grabbed her cell phone out of the rolltop desk in the sitting room. "The service is terrible out here."

His brows furrowed. "I haven't had trouble. Different carriers, I suppose." He ran a hand across his stubbled jaw. He flicked his gaze toward the back door. "Listen, time isn't on our side. Can you go upstairs and lock yourself in a room? I'll call the sheriff."

Heather swallowed hard and grabbed Ruthie's hand. "Come on. Let's go upstairs. I have a dead bolt on my bedroom door." She had installed one there for security for when she opened her house to strangers. She had never dreamed she'd have to use it to keep her ex-husband out.

"What's going on?" Ruthie asked as she be-grudgingly followed her up the stairs, her boots pounding up each step.

When they reached her bedroom, Heather ushered Ruthie inside and spun around, slammed the door and turned the bolt. Why did she think a flimsy lock on a hollow wood door would keep out Brian when a maximum-security prison had failed?

Zach waited at the bottom of the stairs until he heard the bedroom door close and the bolt slide into place. He made a quick call to the sheriff's department. Pulling his gun out of its holster, he moved toward the back door and muttered, "I'm coming to get you, Fox. You're not going to get away from me now."

He exited through the kitchen door, where he had first run into Heather last night. He prayed the sheriff and his deputies didn't take their time in getting here. Zach feared if he picked the wrong outbuilding, Fox might be able to make his escape while he was otherwise occu-pied. Or worse—make his way into the house through the construction zone. To Heather.

After Zach cleared the shed, he heard sirens growing closer. One patrol car pulled up the driveway. Two others sped past before coming to a stop somewhere out of view on the other side of the house. A call like his had probably gotten the attention of the entire Quail Hollow Sheriff's Department.

A tall man unfolded from his patrol car, his hand hovering over the grip of his gun. Zach waved to him silently and pointed to the barn. The man in turn gestured to his officers. The four men surrounded the barn under Zach's silent directions. Two stayed outside watching for any sign of the fugitive while the tall officer and Zach checked the interior. Thanks to several missing planks and a large hole in the roof, most of the interior was well illuminated except for a few dark corners.

Zach cautiously checked the shadows behind a tractor with no rubber on its wheels, an old shell of an Amish buggy and a few hay bales that smelled ripe from dampness and age.

"Clear," he hollered after checking the last stall, where horses must have been kept at some point in the past.

The two law enforcement officers exited the barn together.

"You really think the fugitive made it all the way to Quail Hollow?" The officer looked at his watch as if that might give him the answers. "Isn't Peters Correctional Facility about a hundred miles from here? Guy had to have resources to get to Quail Hollow so quickly."

"He's determined. And he's had help," Zach said bluntly. He offered his hand, introducing himself.

The officer shook his hand. "I'm Deputy Conner Gates. Tell me. Why Quail Hollow? We're a small Amish community."

Zachary glanced up at the house and he saw Heather standing in the upstairs window. This had been her chance at a fresh start after the mayhem Fox had unleashed on her. Yet Fox had found her again and was toying with her.

Zach wasn't going to let this jerk get to Heather. He hadn't been able to save his sister, but he was going to make sure nothing happened to Heather Miller.

"The escapee knows the owner of this property. She testified against him." Zach paused a half second. "And Heather is Brian Fox's ex-wife."

"Oh, man." Gates planted his hand on his hip.

"What makes you believe he's actually here?"

"He left some graffiti on the wall of the residence. He's close."

"Okay," the sheriff's deputy said, "I'll call it

in. We have to immediately make plans. Grid the area. Fan the search out from here."

Zach held his hand up. "Don't let me hold you up. My job is to secure Heather Miller. Keep her safe."

"Heather Miller, you say?" The sheriff's deputy rubbed his jaw. "I didn't realize she had moved back. Shame what happened to her mother."

Zach plowed a hand through his hair. He hated to ask. Apparently he didn't have to, because the officer continued, "My father was sheriff back when her mother was murdered. Heather and her sisters were just little girls. Her father moved away from Quail Hollow with his three daughters and never looked back."

"Can't say I blame him. It's a small town. Everywhere he turned must have reminded him of his wife." Unease twisted his insides. He hadn't realized Heather had so much tragedy in her past.

"They left everything, including their Amish community."

Zach did a double take. "Heather grew up Amish?"

Deputy Gates nodded. "Sure did. Her mother's murder turned this entire town upside down."

* * *

Heather stepped away from the bedroom window, her nerves humming from all the law enforcement activity on her quiet little farm.

Not so quiet anymore.

"I'm sorry you had to get caught in the middle of this," Heather said as she crossed the room to Ruthie, who was sitting quietly in the chaise lounge Heather had put in the corner of the bedroom where she'd envisioned herself escaping with a good book. Not escaping from her fugitive ex-husband.

"Can you tell me what's going on now?" Ruthie dragged her fingers down the edges of her apron over and over. "We have lots of work to do before the bed-and-breakfast opens."

"It looks like everything is safe. For now." From the upstairs window, it looked as if Zach and the sheriff's department had come up empty-handed.

"What is going on? Who is this person they're searching for?" Ruthie's eyes grew wide as she searched Heather's face for answers.

Heather lowered herself onto the edge of the chair and met Ruthie's wary gaze. How did she tell her Amish friend that her ex-husband had escaped prison and had tracked her down in Quail Hollow?

Wasn't this part of the reason the Amish

lived separate from the world? There was too much evil out there. Case in point.

Living the Amish way hadn't saved her mother.

"You deserve the whole truth." Heather swallowed hard and ran her hands up and down her thighs. "A long time ago, I was married to a man who turned out to be abusive."

"This man they're looking for?" Ruthie stopped fidgeting with her apron and stared at her. The fear and uncertainty in her eyes made Heather feel like she had somehow betrayed her friend.

Heather nodded in response to Ruthie's question. "I got away from him—" she fast-forwarded ten years, not wanting to weigh Ruthie down with her past "—but he remarried and killed his second wife."

A quiet gasp escaped Ruthie's lips as blotches of pink fired in her fair-skinned cheeks.

"The man you met downstairs isn't a friend of mine. He's actually a law enforcement officer. Deputy U.S. Marshal Zachary Walker came here to warn me that my ex-husband had escaped prison and was on his way to hurt me."

"I'm so sorry this has happened to you," Ruthie said. "How can I help?"

Heather's breath hitched before she caught herself. This wasn't the response she had expected. Shock, maybe. Questions, definitely. But sympathy and a show of support? Perhaps Ruthie had more exposure to the harsh realities of the outside world than Heather had realized.

"I'd completely understand if you decided you didn't want to work here." Heather felt it necessary to offer her young friend a way out. She couldn't put her in danger.

"I've been looking forward to working here," Ruthie said softly. "It's a pleasant change from the greenhouse."

A knock sounded on the door followed by Zach Walker's authoritative voice. "Fox is gone. It's safe. Come on out."

Heather brushed the back of her hand across Ruthie's sleeve and smiled. She stood and crossed the room to unlock the door. Hoping she could mask her apprehension, she squared her shoulders before opening it.

"We can talk downstairs," Zach said, all business.

Heather led the way downstairs followed by Ruthie, Zach trailing behind.

"It's safe?" Heather repeated his words, although she doubted she'd ever feel safe. She should have never believed she could. As long as there was evil out there—namely Brian Fox—she'd never feel safe again.

Once they reached the new addition, Zach

widened his stance and crossed his arms, looking down at her. "It won't be safe here for you until Fox is back in custody. That's nonnegotiable. You need someplace secure to go for the duration."

"For the duration?" Heather's mind spun. She hated the high-pitched quality of her voice. "I can't just leave. I'm in the middle of renovations. The workmen should be here any minute." Even as she said the words, she realized how ridiculous she sounded. Of course she couldn't stay here. Brian had already found her. Tingles of panic bit at her fingertips and threatened to spread up her arms and consume her with the all-too-familiar fight-or-flight response.

She turned her back to Zach, trying to hide the red flush heating her face. She needed time to think.

The sound of a few Amish workmen speaking in Pennsylvania Dutch floated in from the backyard through the plastic lining covering the opening for the window that was yet to be installed. "I should offer them coffee."

"I'll get the coffee." Ruthie hurried past her and into the kitchen.

"Can we sit down?" Zach asked. "Talk about this?"

Heather had long passed the point of trying to ignore this entire nightmare. She held out her hand, directing him toward the sitting room. Two rockers sat in front of a wood-burning stove, where the tourists were supposed to relax after a day of sightseeing. Not where she was supposed to discuss her ex-husband, who had escaped from prison.

This is too crazy to comprehend. Like a nightmare come true.

The U.S. Marshal leaned forward and rested his elbows on his knees. "You are one of the strongest women I know. It took a lot for you to come forward to testify against Fox in my sister's trial. I'm grateful."

Her stomach twisted at the personal nature of his comment. After she escaped, Brian had killed *Zach's sister*. Zach didn't owe her his gratitude. If she had been braver sooner...

"I didn't have a choice but to testify." She measured her words, fighting back a groundswell of emotion, guilt riding the crest. If she hadn't escaped from Brian, he might not have killed his sister.

You would have been the one he killed...

Heather dragged a hand across her hair and blinked her gritty eyes. Every fiber of her being ached with exhaustion. Frustration. Regret.

"I've put everything into this place. I have

nowhere else to go." Even she could hear the fight draining from her argument.

"The sheriff's deputy told me you have two sisters."

"How did he…? Of course…" Heather slowly shook her head. Quail Hollow was a small town. Despite having kept to herself—except for getting to know Ruthie's family—since she moved into a nearby apartment to start renovations, the residents still knew her story. She didn't truly believe she could be a Miller in Quail Hollow and not have people know about her past, but she had hoped to live a quiet life. *So much for that.* "I can't move in with one of my sisters. I'm not going to put either of them in danger. I can't."

"A relative. Someone Fox doesn't know about."

"My father moved us away from our family. We've lost all ties. Last I heard, my two uncles and their families moved to another Amish community. I suppose I'm the only Miller foolish enough to live in Quail Hollow."

"Friends?"

"I never stayed anywhere long enough to establish friendships. And the friends I had before…"

Pulse thudding in her ears, she slowly turned to meet Zach's steady gaze. "I was married to the man. He knows everything about me. I'm not safe *anywhere*." Her voice cracked over the last word.

"You may feel that way, but I can take you to a safe house."

"You're asking me to run?"

"I know." The look of compassion in his eyes spoke volumes. He knew what he was asking her to do.

"What will happen to this place when I'm gone? If I run, Brian wins. Again." She bowed her head and threaded her fingers through her hair and tugged, frustrated. But even as she made the argument, her resolve was fading.

"It's only temporary." His smooth, calming voice washed over her. If only she could believe that.

"I hid for ten years from Brian." She lifted her gaze, wondering if he could read in her eyes the blame she felt for not coming forward. For not stopping Brian before he had a chance to meet, marry and then kill Zach's sister. As irrational as that thought was, it always came back around to haunt her. In the long chain that had connected Brian Fox to Zach's sister, Jill, she had been a pivotal link.

"The difference this time is that every law enforcement agency in New York State is searching for this guy. It *will* be temporary. He's not living as a free man."

"You can stay with me."

Both Zach and Heather spun around to find Ruthie walking into the sitting room holding two mugs of coffee. "You'll be safe at my home."

"I couldn't," Heather said, accepting the coffee from her Amish friend.

"Wait," Zach said, "that's not a bad idea. Fox wouldn't know to search for you there. You've only recently become friends, right? There's no way Fox would make the connection."

"*Yah*, well, my *mem* and Heather's *mem* were friends a long time ago."

"I can't imagine Fox would connect the dots," Zach said.

"I can't put Ruthie in danger."

"No one will know you're there." Ruthie's eyes shone brightly, the eagerness of only the young and the innocent. "You can even wear my Amish clothes. We're about the same size."

Heather's eyes widened at the young woman's suggestion. Heather might have thought Ruthie had watched a lot of TV to come up with such a crazy plan, but that obviously wasn't the case. She was just a clever young woman.

Zach leaned forward, resting his forearms on

his thighs. His golf shirt stretched across his broad chest. "It's not a bad idea."

"You live with your parents?" Zach asked.

"My *mem*. My *dat* died last year. Now it's just the three of us. I have four older sisters, all married and living nearby. My little sister is fifteen."

"I can't imagine your mother would be happy with having an outsider in her home." Maryann had been nothing but kind and welcoming to Heather, but she wasn't so sure about this. This involved some level of deceit: pretending to be Amish. Would Ruthie's mother go for it?

Ruthie planted her hands on her hips. "She won't mind. My *mem* and your *mem* were best friends. She'd want to help you. I know it."

Surprise trapped a response in Heather's throat.

Zach pushed to his feet. "It's worth asking."

A throbbing started in Heather's temples. "What if he follows us there? I can't…I just can't."

FOUR

Zachary paced the small space between the rocking chairs and the wood-burning stove. "We can take extra precautions to make sure Fox doesn't follow us back to Ruthie's home."

Heather stared up at him, worry lining her pretty eyes. "I don't think this is a good idea."

"I'm not letting you stay here." Zach winced at the way he'd framed the words. He suspected Heather wouldn't take kindly to being forced to do anything. He stopped pacing and sat down on the rocker across from hers. "Don't get me wrong. I'm not going to force you into anything. However, it's against my better judgment and all my training to leave you here. Fox has been here." He pointed in the general direction of the graffiti on the wall. "Please let me—" he looked at Ruthie "—let *us* help you."

He shifted to catch Ruthie's attention. "Do you know the workmen here?"

"*Yah*, Sloppy Sam is a *gut* friend."

"Sloppy Sam?" Zachary couldn't help but smile. Then he turned to Heather. "You hired someone named Sloppy Sam to do home renovations? Seems like a risky move."

Shrugging, Heather mirrored his smile and flicked a quick glance at Ruthie. "Sloppy Sam came highly recommended."

"A lot of Amish have nicknames because so many people have the same name. I know—" Ruthie lifted her hands and held up her fingers. "I know at least seven Samuels. And trust me, Sloppy Sam is a very fine craftsman. He got his nickname when he was a little boy. He tended to enjoy his meals so much that his father kept calling him sloppy. It stuck."

"Well, maybe Sloppy Sam can give you a ride home in his wagon. You can talk to your mother, run the plan by her, then I'll see to it that Heather makes it there, albeit in a circuitous route. Sound like a plan?"

"Yah."

"Please don't tell Sloppy Sam or any of the other Sams you know. The fewer people who know where Heather is, the better."

"I understand." Ruthie pointed toward the back window. "I'll see that the workmen install the window before I leave. Make sure no one else can get in."

Zach met Heather's gaze. She knew as well

as he did that no one could stop a determined Fox from getting in.

"Thank you," Heather said. "You've been a good friend. But please, if I arrive and your mother doesn't want me in her home, please tell me. I don't want to put your family out."

"It'll be fine. You'll see." Ruthie smiled and went outside to talk to the workmen.

"Why don't you grab a few things? I'll drive you to the sheriff's department, and then we'll make alternate plans to get you to Ruthie's house. I don't want Fox to follow us from here."

Heather dragged the charm back and forth across the gold chain on her necklace. "How long do you think it will take before they capture Brian?"

Zach rubbed the back of his neck. "I understand Fox has a lot of experience surviving in the woods. He was big into camping, right?"

Heather nodded. An expression suggesting she was remembering an unhappy camping trip flitted across her features.

"He's more equipped than most to make a go of it out in the woods."

Heather's shoulders sagged, as if she had lost some of her initial bravado. "Do you think I'm foolish to stay in Quail Hollow? Maybe I should put more distance between us."

Zachary leaned forward and reached out to

take her hand, but stopped short of touching her. "You can go round and round with this. I think our initial plan is a good one. We can re-evaluate if either I or the sheriff's department feels your safety is compromised."

Heather raised her eyebrows. "You're not leaving Quail Hollow? I thought your job was to make sure I'm secure."

"It is. And the only way you'll be one hundred percent secure is if Fox is back in custody. Until then, I'm sticking close by."

Heather closed her eyes and shook her head. "I'll grab a bag. It won't take me long. I haven't even had a chance to unpack since moving in here."

The hammering of the workmen clashed with the pounding in Heather's head as she jogged up the stairs to grab a few things. Between the lack of sleep and her plans for the future crashing down around her, she wondered why she had ever allowed herself to dream. To hope for the future.

Tragedy followed her as if she had a flashing neon arrow over her head.

Rely on your faith. Her father's words drifted through her mind. Despite losing his wife and the only life he'd ever known, her father had raised his three daughters to be strong in their faith. To not let their circumstances weigh them down. That God would provide.

Yet her father had worked the last twenty years of his life in a dark factory and died of a heart attack on the way home to his two youngest daughters while riding a public bus during a snowstorm. Help hadn't arrived in time to save him.

God had not provided, but Heather refused to allow that to shatter her faith. She owed that much to her father.

Heather snatched her sweater off the back of the chaise lounge in her bedroom and crammed it into a bag.

Time to go. Hide from Brian. Again.

Her heart ached with the reality that she had come so far only to be pulled back by the man who had always been determined to keep her under his thumb.

"I'll be back," she whispered to her cozy bedroom. That was a promise. She turned and hustled down the stairs. When she reached the bottom, Zach extended a hand to take her bag. "Is this it?"

Heather tipped her head. "I don't suppose I'll be needing much, considering I'll be wearing Ruthie's wardrobe."

Lifting the strap of her bag over his shoulder, he shot her a look she couldn't quite read. "I talked to the workmen. They'll finish up here and Ruthie's going to lock up on her way out."

"And there's no way Brian will follow us to Ruthie's?" Unease twisted her stomach. "I can't—"

"You'll have to trust me on this. Come on." With a hand to the small of her back, he led her outside. His intense scrutiny of their surroundings both comforted and unnerved her. They walked down the muddy driveway, made uneven by the horses' hooves and the narrow wheels of the workmen's wagons.

Alarm coursed through her. "My sisters. They must have heard that Brian escaped. They'll be worried." She dragged her hand across her forehead. The intensity of the morning sun made her feel queasy. "You don't think he'd go after them?"

"He's here. He's coming for you."

She couldn't help but laugh, an awkward, nervous sound. "Is that supposed to make me feel better?"

Half his mouth quirked into a grin. During the trial, she had never seen him so much as crack a smile. "I didn't mean…"

Heather held up her hand. "I know what you meant. But do you think I could contact my sisters? At least let them know I'm okay and to tell them to be more cautious. To report anything suspicious."

"Of course. We can make a few phone calls from the sheriff's office before I take you to Ruthie's home." He quickened his pace, nudging her forward with a hand to her elbow. "But let's get you off this property."

Heather squinted against the sun and tented her hand over her eyes. "Where did you park?" He was leading her across the narrow country road.

"I parked behind the buggy here. I didn't want to draw attention to my vehicle in case Fox was watching."

Still holding her elbow, he led her around the buggy and they both came up short. Her stomach bottomed out and she willed away her urgent need to throw up. The windshield of his truck had been smashed.

With two hands on her waist, Zach set her next to the buggy like she was a child who needed to be told to stay put and not move. He reached for his gun. "Stay here." He set her bag down on the gravel lot.

A flush of dread washed over her and she struggled to catch her breath. She glanced around, her vision narrowing. A crow silently flapped its wings overhead, cutting a path across the sky.

The cornfields swayed in the winds. The sweet scent of corn and dried leaves reached her nose.

A split-rail fence in need of repair.

A long-ago abandoned silo.

Yesterday, this landscape had brought her peace. Today she saw nothing but places for Brian to hide.

She flexed and relaxed her hands, trying to tamp down her panic. He was not going to destroy her life. Not again.

Leaning over, she scooped up the strap of her bag that Zach had dropped and waited. She glanced around to make sure they were alone. Zach did the same as he strode across the gravel lot.

After a closer inspection of his vehicle, he walked back toward her, all the while keeping a watchful eye on the landscape. His posture relaxed. Perhaps he was convinced the immediate threat had passed. Something made him go back to the vehicle and open his driver's door. He paused. A muscle ticked in his jaw. He stepped away from the open door with an envelope in his hand.

"What's that?" Despite her best efforts to be strong, her voice trembled.

"It's addressed to you." But he didn't hand it to her. They made eye contact briefly before he pulled out a pocket knife and slid the blade under the seal of the envelope.

Another crow cawed overhead as he pulled out a piece of paper and unfolded it. The edges flapped in the wind. She stepped closer, wanting to read the note. *Not* wanting to read the note. Blinking rapidly, her eyes watered from staring at the bright white paper in the blinding sunshine. The wavy black lines came into focus: "You can run. But you can't hide."

She let out a long breath between tight lips. She recognized Brian's handwriting. The same meticulous letters that he'd carved into notes giving her instructions on what to buy for dinner or how to wear her hair or when to be home. Or how to wash his clothes, hang his pants, fold his socks. His demanding directives had been as particular as they were plentiful.

He'd controlled her.

Heather's stomach twisted and she feared she would have thrown up if not for her empty stomach.

"I wonder why he left the note in my truck and not in your house. He had access." Zach turned the note over in his hand.

Heather turned her back to the truck, suddenly sensing they were not alone. "He wanted me to know that even you can't keep me safe."

* * *

Zach slammed his fist on the frame of the door of his truck and muttered under his breath. "We're going to have to get a sheriff to take us to their office."

"My car is parked behind the barn."

"No, it's better if we don't take your car. Too obvious." Just then, he looked up and saw Deputy Gates walking toward his patrol car. He waved to the man. Gates climbed into his vehicle and drove over, pulling up alongside his damaged truck. The officer rolled down his window. "What happened here?"

"Fox got to my truck. He might be hiding in the cornfields." Zach kept Heather close as he scanned his surroundings. He tapped the roof of the sheriff's patrol car. "Forget about my truck for now. I can get someone to tow it to a collision shop. I need to get Miss Miller out of here. All this open space is giving me the willies."

He thought he heard Heather mutter, "The willies?" under her breath.

"Can you take us to the sheriff's department?"

The deputy tipped his head toward the back of his vehicle. "Hop in."

Zach held out his hand for Heather. Hesitancy flashed in her eyes before she climbed in.

He suspected not many people liked to travel in the back of a patrol car. He ran around and jumped in the front passenger seat.

Zach looked over his shoulder and smiled at Heather sitting in the backseat. "We'll get you to safety."

She stared at him with a blank expression in her eyes, seemingly unconvinced.

"Nice to meet you, Miss Miller. I'm Deputy Conner Gates. I hear you're opening a bed-and-breakfast in your grandmother's house," the deputy said casually to Heather as he pulled out onto the road.

"Yeah…" She stretched the word out, as if she were about to ask him how he knew her plans, but then realized word traveled quickly in a small town. "I hope to open in less than two weeks. I already have it booked."

"The fall foliage is beautiful. Our little hotel in town can't keep up with the tourists. You'll have a booming business, I'm sure." The deputy was good at making small talk, obviously trying to distract Heather from the events going on around her.

"That's what I was counting on," Heather said, noncommittally. Defeat slipped into her tone, as if her dreams had been forever dashed by today's events.

"The town will be happy to see the old house

come to life again." The deputy flicked his gaze into the rearview mirror and Zach could imagine Heather smiling back politely.

"How far is the sheriff's office?" Zach asked, determined to get the focus off Heather.

"In the center of town. Ten-minute drive. From there, we'll get an unmarked vehicle to take Miss Miller to a safe location."

"I have something else in mind. Something Fox would never expect." Zach tapped the door handle, nervous energy from the adrenaline surging through his veins.

"Whatever you say," the deputy said.

Cornfields whizzed past in a blur. A flash of something dark emerged from the cornfields just ahead, catching Zach's eye and making his pulse spike. He held up his hand, as if that would stop the car. "Slow down."

Before the deputy slowed, the form—dressed in black—crouched low on the side of the road.

"Get down!" Zach yelled. "Get down!"

The back window shattered with an explosive sound. The patrol car skidded, weaved, then picked up speed.

The deputy scrambled for the radio controls. "Shooter on Lapp Road. In the cornfields point five miles from the Miller home. Patrol car's been hit. Send backup."

"Stay down," Zach yelled as he tried to

stay hunkered down and get a location on the shooter. A ping sounded somewhere else on the vehicle. He cursed under his breath. "Stay down." He stretched his hand over the seat and touched Heather's head. She had unbuckled and taken refuge in the tight space behind the front seat.

After another half mile, Zach was confident the shooter had retreated into the cornfields. "Pull over."

The deputy did as Zach instructed. Zach climbed out and yanked open the back door, his heart racing in his chest. "Heather, Heather! Are you okay?"

Heather sat up, terror radiating in her bright brown eyes. He reached out and raked the shards of glass from her hair. "Are you hit?"

She pressed her hand to her chest. "I... No... no, I'm okay."

"Okay." Zach gritted his jaw in determination. He closed her car door, then leaned into the front passenger seat. "Take her to the sheriff's office. I'm going after him."

Without waiting for the deputy to finish his protest, Zach slammed the door and patted the roof. "Go!" Grabbing his gun from its holster, he ran back in the direction of the shooter, his senses on high alert.

Every twig snap, bird crow and rustling stalk sent his adrenaline spiking over the edge.

Fox. It had to be Fox. He couldn't let him get away.

Breathing hard, Zach reached the point where the gunman had emerged from the cornfields, and based on the footprints, the same point where he had ducked back into them. Zach had also noted the mile marker.

Pulse whooshing in his ears, he slowed, cautious not to get ambushed, fearing his need to get revenge might override his better judgment.

Examining the ground, he noticed a heavy boot print in the dirt. Sliding between the cornstalks, he followed the prints, the deeper in, the less certain the path of travel, but they seemed to be leading to woods on the other side of the fields.

Once he reached the woods, he slowed, trying to quiet his ragged breath. In the distance, he heard water, a river or creek. Pausing a moment, he let his eyes adjust to the heavily shadowed woods, except for the occasional beam of bright sunlight that penetrated the thick canopy.

Gun in hand, he made his way deeper into the woods, toward the sound of water. Once he got to the clearing, he caught sight of a man on a dock, leaning over something. A boat, maybe?

Zach raced toward the dock.

"Fox!"

The man spun around and fired without warning. Zach dived behind a tree, then shot back from the protection of his hiding place.

Another shot split the bark near his shoulder.

"You've run out of options. Drop the weapon," Zach yelled, sensing perhaps his statement contradicted his current predicament.

Another shot rang out, this one spraying the dirt at his feet.

Pressing flat against the tree, he yelled, "Fox. You've got nowhere to go. Drop your weapon. Surrender."

"Surrender? And go back to that hellhole?" Fox yelled back, his voice slightly muffled. "No way."

The sound of an engine ripped through the still air. Zach's chest tightened as he peered out from behind the safety of the tree. Fox was on a boat motoring away from the end of the dock. The water in the creek rushed from last night's rain.

Pulse pounding in his ears, Zach sprinted to the dock, the soles of his shoes sucking into the muck on the shore. The boat was about thirty feet away from the dock with the distance quickly growing.

Zach planted his feet and took aim at the man who had murdered his sister.

FIVE

The edge of the hard plastic chair bit into the back of Heather's thighs as she waited impatiently for U.S. Marshal Zachary Walker to return. That was how she had to think of him, as U.S. Marshal Zachary Walker, professional law enforcement officer, because if she made it personal, it made her worry too much. She couldn't imagine the bravery it took to charge after Brian Fox, her ex-husband-slash-convict.

She'd never be able to live with herself if he got hurt—*or worse*—because of her.

No, not because of you, a more rational voice whispered to her. But it was hard to separate the two. Brian Fox was in Quail Hollow because of her.

Leaning forward, she focused all her nervous energy on plucking out the shards of glass that had rained down on her as she hunkered down in the backseat of the patrol car. If Zach hadn't hollered out his warning, would her ex-husband finally have made good on his promise to kill her?

Groaning, she stood and dumped the shards she had collected in the palm of her hand into the garbage. She paced the small office area. She promised Deputy Conner Gates she wouldn't wander away because anywhere beyond the protection of law enforcement she was liable to become target practice once again for her ex-husband. Given another chance, he wouldn't miss.

The deputy had been called away ten minutes ago and she sent up a silent prayer that U.S. Marshal Zachary Walker had apprehended Brian and he was headed back to Peters Correctional Facility. But no one seemed to want to tell her what was going on.

A bustling at the door drew her attention. Deputy Gates entered followed by the U.S. Marshal.

Thank God. Zachary is safe.

She tamped down her initial reaction to gush all over him, to express her relief that he was safe.

Their relationship was strictly professional.

So why did she care so much about his safe return? Probably because she couldn't handle knowing her ex-husband had hurt another person. He had to be stopped.

Zach made his way to her. She had already given up the pretense of his official title. She lowered her gaze. Mud caked the bottom and sides of his shoes. A deep scratch lined the back of his left hand.

"You okay?" he asked, his mood somber.

"Yeah. Did you get him?" Her pulse whooshed in her ears and she feared she wouldn't hear the answer.

"No." The apology in his eyes said far more than the single word.

Her stomach plummeted. "He got away." She dragged a hand through her hair and her fingers got tangled in the snarled mess. She spun around and glanced up, refusing to cry.

"We exchanged gunfire. Then he climbed into a boat on the creek," Zach explained. "I got off another shot before he disappeared around a bend. I'm confident I hit him, but I couldn't stop him." His monotone voice suggested even he was having trouble accepting the turn of events.

"You shot him? But he got away?" she repeated in disbelief.

"They're searching the creek. There's no way he'll get far."

She slowly lowered herself onto the familiar plastic chair. "So…what? We wait here until they bring him in?"

Zach sat down next to her and tipped his head to meet her gaze. "The deputy and I think we should move forward with our plan to take you to Ruthie's house. And with an abundance of caution, we'll take a circuitous route to make sure no one follows."

"But if he's…" She couldn't say the word *dead*. Did she really wish him dead? God forgive her. She didn't want him dead—she just wanted him safely behind bars.

Zach gently rubbed his knuckles across the back of her hand. She expected the urge to flee would overwhelm her, make her feel trapped—like it always had when someone got too close—but instead, an unexpected warmth spread up her arm. "Until we've located Fox, we can't take any chances," he said, his voice hoarse.

"You hit him?"

"Yes, I'm sure I did. But he only cranked the motor to full throttle. I was at a disadvantage on the shore."

"Your shoes."

He lifted his boot. "Good thing I had my hiking boots at my cabin."

"Your cabin?"

Zach crossed his arms and tucked his hands under his armpits and he seemed to stifle a shudder. He was probably freezing after running through the cornfields. "Yeah, I have a cabin in Quail Hollow. I had just arrived last night when my supervisor called to alert me of the situation."

Realization twisted her stomach. "If you hadn't come to my property, Brian might have gotten to me first." The image of the graffiti on the wall in her newly constructed eating area was etched in her brain. "Why didn't he attack me when he had the chance? He was in my house." Her lips grew numb with fear and she had trouble forming the words.

"I think he wanted to toy with you, but law enforcement descended too quickly."

The thought of her being terrorized—again—by her ex-husband made her realize she might never be free from this man.

Unless he's dead.

Zach reached out and gently touched her knee as if he recognized the turmoil she was in. "Will you let me take you to Ruthie's? We'll wait until dark. I promise I'll keep you safe."

Heather nodded. She didn't put much stock in promises, but with Brian most likely mortally wounded, she figured Zach's promise to keep her safe might be reasonable.

When Heather arrived at Ruthie's home under the cloak of darkness in a delivery van from the local hardware store, she suspected this was how kidnap victims felt. By the time Zach opened the back doors, her backside ached from each and every bump they'd hit between Quail Hollow's town center and Ruthie's family farm. Sitting on the hard metal surface of the back of the delivery fan wasn't exactly the lap of luxury. And the smell of fresh wood and some sort of fertilizer mingled in her nose and coated her mouth.

Zach held out his hand to her. She accepted it and climbed out, grateful to stretch her legs. She couldn't help but smile at Ruthie as she directed Zach and the driver to stack the fertilizer and wood in the barn. "You actually needed this stuff?" he asked.

"Why waste a trip? My *mem* needs supplies for the greenhouse." Maryann Hershberger and her youngest daughter, Emma, as well as her older daughter Ruthie, ran a greenhouse on the property. Heather had befriended the family after she moved to Quail Hollow, drawn to them by a letter Maryann had written to her father years ago. After getting to know them, Heather had hired Ruthie to work at the bed-and-breakfast. Heather suspected the small family needed the extra income working at the bed-and-breakfast would provide.

If they were able to get back to the required work necessary before opening day.

"How did you arrange all this?" Heather asked as she brushed the loose soil from the back of her pants.

Her question was directed to Zach, but Ruthie stepped forward, rolling up on the balls of her black boots. "The deputy reached me on the phone and he asked me if I ever take deliveries from any businesses in town."

Heather held up her hand. "Wait. You have a phone?" Her father had grown up Amish and had taken his young family away from Quail Hollow when Heather was only six. Her sisters had been three and two. He'd told them so many stories about the Amish that'd made the young girls long for a home they were too young to remember.

Ruthie jabbed her thumb in the direction of a pole deeper in the barn. A generator hummed and a soft bulb illuminated a phone mounted on the pole. "The *Ordnung* allows us to have a phone for business purposes as long as it's not in the house. The phone serves a purpose but shouldn't interrupt our daily lives." She smiled, a hint of apology lurking in her eyes. "I have an answering machine here, too. So I can return all the calls I miss. In this case, I was happy the sheriff's department reached out. Now you'll be safe because no one knows you're here."

Zach reached into his pocket and pulled out a business card. "Tack this up near the phone in case you need to reach me."

Ruthie took the card and turned it over in her hand. "I will."

Heather cut a sideways glance at Zach, wondering how much Ruthie really knew. Did she know that Brian had shot at the patrol car? That Zach had chased him through the fields until he escaped by boat, but likely not before he was shot?

"The sheriff's department has been a big help. Thank you," Heather said. She knew they had hoped to limit the number of people who knew her location for security purposes, but she also realized it wasn't feasible.

"Not being from Quail Hollow, I couldn't do this on my own." Zach held out his hand to the young man leaning against the truck. "This gentleman is a deputy." The man tipped his head in acknowledgment.

"Another officer is going to arrange to drop off a truck on one of the nearby back roads for our use in an emergency, since mine is out of commission."

"Looks like you've covered everything," Heather said, dragging a hand through her hair, the exhaustion catching up with her. She hadn't slept well last night and today had been nothing but one stress-inducing event after another.

"My job is to keep you safe," Zach said.

"Well," she said, trying to sound more encouraged than she really felt, "hopefully this mess will be behind us soon and we can all go back to our regularly scheduled lives."

Ruthie grabbed a paper sack and opened it up. "I brought you some clothes."

"Thank you." Heather took the bag and set it in the back of the van. The fabric of the long dress felt heavy as she pulled it out.

"Do you really think this is necessary?" She ran her fingers down the ties of the bonnet.

"It's another layer of protection. I don't think Fox will be looking for an Amish woman."

Heather smoothed her hand down the pale blue fabric and a distant memory fluttered around the periphery of her mind. "I suppose not." She glanced around the open space of the barn. "Am I to get dressed in here?"

"We'll give you privacy." Zach tipped his head to the driver and they both stepped out of the barn.

"Would you like some help?" Ruthie asked. "There are pins to hold it closed."

"Pins?" Heather noticed the metal sparkle in the dull light.

"No buttons allowed."

Heather blinked slowly, unable to wrap her fuzzy brain around all the arbitrary rules. Rules her mother and father both had grown up following.

"Yes, I'd appreciate that."

Ruthie turned her back and Heather slipped off what her friend would call *Englisch* clothes and quickly slipped on the dress. "Okay, ready."

Ruthie spun around and her eyes widened. "Wow, you look… Wait…" She stepped closer and reached for Heather's hair, twisting it back into a low bun. With careful concentration, Ruthie reached into her apron and pulled out some bobby pins and secured her hair. "Almost ready." She stooped and reached into the bag and produced a bonnet. Ruthie secured it on Heather's head and stepped back. "There. You look right nice. Like regular Amish."

Heather touched the bonnet and was eager to see herself in the mirror. She hadn't had time to put makeup on this morning, so she imagined she did look like most other Amish women, even if she didn't feel like one.

Heather pulled up the hem of her dress and examined her purple sneakers. Ruthie laughed—the young woman had such an easygoing nature—and said, "You can always go barefoot. Or I'm sure I can find an old pair of boots."

Before Heather had a chance to comment, Zach hollered from outside the door. "You decent in there?"

Without saying anything, Heather walked to the opening where the truck was still parked, her heart racing in her chest. She felt a little bit like she was going to prom and about to show off her gown to her date, albeit the dress she was wearing was a lot plainer than the pink sparkly one she had worn another lifetime ago.

What Zach didn't say was telegraphed in his eyes. "I guess you're ready."

"Wait a minute," Heather said with feigned annoyance. "What about you? Aren't you supposed to be undercover?"

Zach made a sound she couldn't quite decipher.

Ruthie held up a finger and ran into the barn, then came back with a broad-brimmed felt hat. She handed it to Zach, who stuffed it on his head. "All right, then."

"We can find some of my *dat*'s clothes for you once we get inside."

"Ready?" he asked.

Heather couldn't read the expression in his shadowed eyes. A part of her felt like she was playing dress up, but nothing about this dangerous situation was pretend.

The truck that had provided Heather safe passage had pulled away and Zach escorted her across the farm, past the greenhouse and up the front steps of Ruthie's home. He continuously scanned the surroundings. Far too many places for someone to hide. But they had decided the less police presence here, the better. If Fox had somehow gotten off the creek, they didn't want to send out any red flares as to Heather's location.

Zach blinked slowly as flashes of memory assaulted him. The sound of the shots, the smell of the residue, his own jagged breathing in his ears...

There was no way he'd missed. *No way.* The first few shots he took were defensive shots from behind the safety of the tree. But the last shot, he had Fox in his sights.

As they climbed the front steps, Heather reached up and slipped her hand around the crook of his arm. "Are you sure this is a good idea? I don't want to put anyone else in danger," she whispered as Ruthie opened the door.

"This will all be over soon. I promise."

Heather dropped her hand and smoothed it over her dress.

"You look rather fetching," he said, keeping his voice low while trying to lighten the mood.

"Nice hat," she tossed back at him.

"I might see if we can add it to the U.S. Marshals uniform."

She turned to him and raised her eyebrows. She looked like she was about to say something else when his cell phone rang. Zach glanced at the screen and noticed it was a local call, probably the sheriff's department.

"I better take this. I'll be in shortly." He waited until Ruthie and Heather closed the door behind them. He stepped off the porch and hung in the shadows. "Marshal Walker."

"Hey, it's Gates. I have an update."

Zach held his breath waiting for the words like *body, dead, recovery, it's over*. Instead the local sheriff's deputy said, "We found a boat on the creek with some blood in it. But there's still no sign of Fox."

Zach swallowed hard. "What do you mean?" A thumping started behind his eyes and any hope that this situation was going to be resolved today ebbed out of him.

"The boat was found on the west side of Quail Hollow Creek. It wasn't anchored or tied down. We could speculate a lot from that."

Zach closed his eyes and pushed his hat up

on his head and rubbed his forehead. "He might have fallen out of the boat."

"If that's the case, might take a few more days to find his body."

Zach turned around and glanced at the well-maintained house. A soft light glowed in the front window. He had to reassure himself that Heather was safe, regardless of the bad news.

Just a few more days.

But a niggling in the back of his head made him wonder if it really would be over in a few days. Fox was one tough egg.

"What are the chances Fox got out of the boat and is on the run? How much blood was in the boat?"

"The amount of blood itself didn't indicate a fatal injury, but a wounded prisoner won't make it long in the woods. We'll find him."

"And if he went into the creek?"

"Search teams are scheduled to drag a section of the creek in the morning. Hold tight."

"Will do." Zach ended the call and stood for a few more minutes outside. He drew in a deep breath, trying to calm his rioting emotions. The stillness on the farm was almost eerie.

Brian Fox was not going to get away. Law enforcement would either find him or his body tomorrow, in the light of day. Zach's job was to keep Heather safe in the meantime.

SIX

"Mem!" Ruthie called as she led Heather into her home through a tidy sitting room and toward the back of the house. Every time Heather visited the Hershbergers' home, she was struck by how there wasn't a single framed photo in the room. Maybe she noted it because she regretted that she didn't have any photos of her mother, who grew up in the Amish way. The Amish were forbidden from having their photos taken.

"We're here. I have Heather Miller with me," Ruthie called cheerily, as if she had simply brought home a friend for dinner.

When they reached the kitchen, Mrs. Hershberger put the glass she had been washing into the drying rack and turned to face them. Her mouth opened as if she were about to offer them a greeting, when a look Heather couldn't quite define skated across the older woman's eyes. Her hands flew to her mouth in slow motion. Water rimmed her wide eyes.

"Oh, you look just like your *mem*, Sarah." Mrs. Hershberger walked over slowly to Heather and stopped in front of her. Heather half expected her to touch her face, but Ruthie's mother simply dropped her hands to her sides and studied her intently. "I saw the resemblance before, but now…" She clasped her hands and held them to her chest.

For a moment, any words were trapped in Heather's throat as the walls of the cozy kitchen grew close. She tipped her head and felt the tightness of her hair gathered at the nape of her neck. Finally she found some words. "My father used to tell me that I looked a lot like my mother, but I had never seen a photo of her." Her voice cracked. The fact that the Amish forbade their members from having their photo taken seemed like a harmless enough rule, but when you were a kid whose mom died when you were six, you couldn't help but be a bit resentful. Yet, unbeknownst to her, with each passing year she had apparently grown to resemble her mother.

"I saw the resemblance when you visited before." Mrs. Hershberger had started to repeat what she was saying earlier. "But now, without makeup and with the Amish clothes…"

There was a quiet reverence to the older woman's tone.

"I hardly remember my mom, but I'm honored that you think I look like her. My father said she was a beauty."

Mrs. Hershberger dropped her hands to her sides and pink splotches colored her fair skin. "Oh, forgive me. That was rude. Please come in. Sit down." She pulled a chair out from the long pine table. "Can I get you something? Ruthie tells me you've run into a bit of trouble and need someplace to stay."

Heather's gaze drifted to Ruthie and she wondered how much she had confided in her mom. Mrs. Hershberger deserved the entire truth if she was opening her home up to her.

"Did Ruthie tell you what was going on, Mrs. Hershberger?"

The older woman froze, her well-worked fingers wrapped around the top slat of the back of the chair. "Please, call me Maryann. And yes, Ruthie told me you had an old boyfriend who might try to hurt you."

Heather made eye contact with Ruthie and smiled. Ruthie was both determined and confident, two qualities Heather imagined were not in overabundance in young Amish women—or in young women in general.

"It's more than that. He's actually my ex-husband, who escaped from prison after being sent there for killing his second wife."

Maryann gasped and walked around to the front of the chair and slowly sat down, as if the news had ripped the steel rod from her spine. She sat perched on the edge of the chair, seeming ready to bolt at a moment's notice. "Perhaps my daughter left out a few details."

"I didn't want to be a gossip," Ruthie said, joining them at the table and leaning eagerly forward as if afraid her mother was going to rescind the invitation.

Heather wondered if the woman was more horrified that she had been divorced or that her ex was an escaped convict. She hoped, despite the woman's strong religious convictions, that she wouldn't condemn her for putting her very life above the sanctity of marriage. Heather had long ago made peace with her decision and expected that God would forgive her.

However, during all her previous visits with the Hershbergers, Heather had omitted the darker side of her past. Had she not forgiven herself?

Heather ran the palms of her hands over the edge of the pine table. She imagined that not too long ago, it was surrounded by a big loving family who had now grown and moved on to create happy dinner tables of their own.

The passage of time and her spouse's premature death had left Maryann alone with her youngest two daughters, Ruthie and Emma.

"I'd understand if you'd rather I stay someplace else. My ex-husband is both smart and ruthless."

Ruthie squared her shoulders, the light in her eyes suggesting she rarely had such excitement in her life. "Marshal Walker made sure no one followed Heather here. Precautions were taken. There's no reason to believe we're in danger. Besides, Heather needs someplace safe to stay."

Maryann's gaze drifted toward the front room. "And this law enforcement person—"

"He had to take a phone call. He'll be in in a minute," Ruthie interrupted her mother, obviously determined to convince her that they had to host their *Englisch* friends.

Maryann's lips grew pinched, then relaxed before she spoke again. "He plans to stay here, too?"

Heather caught Ruthie's eye, encouraging her to stay quiet so she could speak. "Yes, if that's okay with you. It'll be safer if he's here. For everyone."

Maryann smoothed the folds in her dress near her thighs. "I do suppose we have the room. But I'll need for both of you to respect our home. No phone calls. No guns."

"Mem," Ruthie groaned, sounding like a typical teenager. "He needs his gun."

Maryann hiked her chin, not about to back down. "He can keep it in the barn."

"Are you sure we're not an imposition? We can make other plans," Heather suggested, even though she wasn't sure what those other plans would be. Her preference was to stay in Quail Hollow, close to the final renovations of her bed-and-breakfast. But those were selfish plans.

"We have invited you into our home. You don't need to make other plans." The finality in Maryann's tone stopped Heather from questioning her host further.

"I'll check on Zach." Heather pushed away from the table. Just then Emma came running down the stairs. She greeted them shyly.

"Excuse me a minute," Heather said, not missing the look of surprise on Ruthie's fifteen-year-old sister's face. On the way to the front door, Heather caught sight of her sneakers poking out from the bottom of her dress.

Pausing at the front door, she listened to see if Zach was still talking on the phone. She didn't want to interrupt. She thought she heard him wrapping up the call. Reaching for the door handle, she said a silent prayer that he'd have good news for her.

Was it wrong to pray that Brian was dead?

Maybe. Perhaps she should pray that he was back in custody instead?

Drawing in a deep breath, she opened the door. Zach turned toward her. The deep lines of concern etched on his handsome face under the moonlight told her that her prayers would have to wait to be answered.

Zach slid his cell phone back into his jacket pocket, then took off his broad-brimmed hat and set it on a small table that sat between two rocking chairs on the front porch.

"That's not the face of a man with good news," Heather said, pulling the front door closed behind her with a quiet click.

He searched her face for a moment. "No, it's not. They still haven't located Fox."

The strings of Heather's white bonnet pooled around the hollow of her neck. Her hand fluttered around the tips of the strings. A part of him wondered if this ruse was being disrespectful to the Amish people of this community. Playing dress up to avoid detection.

"Is it wrong that I hoped he was dead?" Heather whispered.

"You have a right to be frightened." He ran a hand across his jaw. "I'm sorry I didn't catch him earlier, then neither one of us would be standing on this porch pretending we're Amish."

"Hmm…" There was a distant quality to her voice. "I thought being here in the country would be more peaceful. I guess I didn't bargain on Brian escaping from prison."

"None of us could have predicted that."

"I know." She drew in a deep breath. "Hey, listen," she said with a forced cheery tone. "Ruthie's mother is fine with us staying, but she asked that we don't use our phones in her house and she wants you to keep your gun in the barn."

Zach gave his head a quick shake. "Wait. What? I need to be able to protect you." He took a step back, then forward. "No, okay…" He ran the options over in his head. "It's probably better if I patrol the grounds tonight anyway. Yeah, that will work. I'll stay outside."

"You've got to be exhausted. You didn't sleep last night, either."

Zach blinked slowly but refused to admit how tired he was. Regardless of his exhaustion, he wouldn't be able to rest until Fox was no longer a threat.

When he didn't answer, Heather said, "I can keep you company."

He slowly shook his head. "I'd feel better if I knew you were safely inside. I'm going to see if Mrs. Hershberger will allow me to do a quick sweep of the house." He scratched his head. "Please tell me the Amish have locks."

"We have locks."

Both Heather and Zach spun around to find Mrs. Hershberger standing in the doorway. After telling Zach to call her Maryann, she went on to explain that not every Amish home had a lock, but Maryann had insisted her husband put locks on the doors and windows after her dear friend—Heather's mother—had been murdered.

Maryann turned to look Heather in the eye. "We all lost a little something the day your mother was killed. Some far more than others, of course. But many of us who called her friend forever lost a sense of safety."

Heather bowed her head but didn't say anything.

"I'm sorry for your loss," Maryann continued. "I'm not happy about the situation, but I'm grateful I can help my dear friend's daughter."

Until this very moment, Zach hadn't truly considered the amount of loss Heather had suffered over her short life. He had been too focused on his own.

Heather nodded, as if she couldn't spare any words.

"Locks are a good thing," Zach said, needing

to focus on the task at hand. "I have my gun in its holster, but can I do a quick tour of your home, then I'll stay outside?"

"You're going to stay up all night watching the house?"

"That's my job." His gaze drifted to Heather. However, that wasn't entirely true. In just a short time, it was beginning to feel like far more than just a job. He would have thought he'd be able to keep it strictly professional, but something about this woman, even dressed in plain clothing, made him wonder... No, this *was* just a job. Even if he did enjoy Heather's company, he would never be able to see her without thinking of his sister. Who wanted to live life with those constant reminders?

Maryann clasped her hands. "Okay, you can come in the house with your gun." She pressed her hands together. "But, please, I don't want to see it. You can take one of the guest rooms. You need to protect Heather. Her mother and I were best friends."

"I appreciate that." Zach grabbed his hat from where he'd set it down. They all went inside the house and he personally saw to it that all the doors and windows were secured.

Long after the women retired upstairs, he stood in the dark sitting room staring out the window wondering if Fox was still stalking his way through Quail Hollow or if he lay dying deep in the woods. Or if his body had sunk to the bottom of the creek.

None of the ideas brought him peace. Nothing would bring him peace until he knew for sure that Fox could no longer hurt anyone.

One of the advantages of staying at a true Amish home was that Heather had been unable to watch TV and see what she assumed was the relentless, round-the-clock coverage of a convict on the run playing out over all the local news networks. However, her sisters had been inundated with the news and were wildly relieved when Heather reached out to them. She assured them she was safe, but couldn't share the details. They also had strict instructions to call the police if they noticed anything suspicious.

Over the course of the few days that she and Zach were at the Hershbergers' home, Zach had given Heather occasional news updates—editing out any parts that may have included her, per her request—but the only update she really wanted was the one that reported her ex-husband was back in custody.

Or dead.

Feeling a little stir-crazy as a light drizzle made the autumn day bleak, Heather got up from the breakfast table with plans to retreat to the solitude of the greenhouse to water the mums. Zach had excused himself a while ago to make phone calls on the front porch.

Heather cleared her dishes, then went out the back door. As she crossed the muddy driveway, she was again grateful Ruthie had found an old pair of boots for her.

She opened the glass door to the greenhouse and stepped inside. The temperature was cranked high, but it felt good on this damp, dreary day. She found she enjoyed working in the greenhouse. The Hershbergers sold plants and flowers to the public. On Sunday, a lot of non-Amish customers stopped by to purchase hay bales, mums and dried cornstalks for autumn decorations. Zach had insisted he and Heather stay inside. Out of sight. But once Monday, Tuesday and now Wednesday rolled around, the visitors dried up. Apparently the greenhouse was a weekend business patronized by tourists out for a country drive.

Zach had decided it was safe for Heather to stroll the property—not that Brian would be looking for his ex-wife dressed in traditional Amish clothing. She spent time in the greenhouse: watering the mums, deadheading the plants and general organizing. It afforded her the simple luxury of expending some of her nervous energy. Sometimes Ruthie or Emma came with her, keeping her thoughts occupied with things other than Brian Fox. She enjoyed listening to their chatter.

"There you are. I'm not going to want you to leave," Maryann said, stepping inside the greenhouse and picking up the garden gloves from the nearby shelf. Then her eyes widened. "I probably shouldn't have said that. I meant—"

Heather smiled. "No need to explain. Once I get the bed-and-breakfast up and running, I should make time for gardening. It's relaxing."

"Your mother used to say the same thing."

Heather met Maryann's gaze. "My mother liked to garden?" If Maryann wasn't such a kind, genuine soul, Heather might have been embarrassed by the raw desire to learn about her mother. Like a child eager to hear every last bit about the day-to-day life of Santa Claus.

"Oh, she loved to garden. She used to bring you and your sisters here on occasion, not that she had much free time while caring for her growing family and running a household. But she was the one who suggested we start a greenhouse."

Heather should have suspected considering her name and those of her sisters, Lily and Rose.

Maryann continued talking. "My husband

had fallen ill and farming was getting tough. This was something I could do with my daughters." Maryann adjusted the band of her glove. "My husband was sick for many years. Now it's just me and the two youngest girls."

The water from the hose was pooling at Heather's feet as she listened to the story, realizing her mother had probably stood exactly where she stood. Used the same hose. Felt the heat from the glass enclosure. She tried to still the moment, capture it, but curiosity got the best of her. "What do you know about my mother's death?"

The color drained from Maryann's face and Heather quickly added, "My father never talked about it and there's not a lot of information online."

"Online?" Maryann narrowed her eyes in confusion. Some of the younger Amish may have been familiar with their worldly neighbors' ways, but obviously Maryann had no exposure to computers or the lingo.

"I did a search on my computer. People can pull up old news articles. I learned that she was murdered and that she was found in the barn on my *mammy*'s farm." A flush of dread washed over her. She hadn't spoken out loud about her mother's murder since the day she was fifteen and had asked her dad about it. He'd shut her down in no uncertain terms. His grief had been so palpable that she hadn't dared ask him again. Now it was too late because he had passed away years ago.

Then a few years later, she met Brian and things spiraled out of control from there. Heather had been so fixated on protecting herself that she hadn't had time to reflect on the past. Only after Brian's incarceration did Heather feel that maybe she could reclaim some of her past. Figure out who she was. What she had lost all those years ago.

"The news articles were pretty vague." Heather studied Maryann's face, not wanting to rehash the tragic incident. "I imagine not many of the Amish wanted to talk to the newspapers or the police."

Maryann lifted her hand and shook her head. "I have tried to put it out of my memory." She pressed her lips together. "It was a long time ago. Maybe it's best if you forget."

"How can I forget something that shaped who I am? If my *mem* hadn't been murdered, I would have grown up in this Amish community. My entire life would have been different. Please, tell me what you remember."

Maryann peeled back the lid from a container of fertilizer and focused intently on scooping out the contents, then dumping the small beads into the pot of a mum, bursting with pretty purple buds.

Finally Maryann dropped the scoop back into the container and tore off her gardening gloves. She slumped back, resting a hip against the metal table. "The person who hurt your mother was an outsider. He was never caught." She looked up. "Don't ruin your future by searching the past. There are no answers. You must forgive him in your heart. He will be judged by God."

Maryann had grown somber and Heather regretted bringing up her mom's murder. If she couldn't have answers about her death, at least she wanted to know who her *mem* was in life. She decided to bring up the subject of her mother's life at another time.

A quiet knock sounded on the door. The two women turned to see Zach opening the glass door to the greenhouse. He wore black pants and a black shirt—most likely purchased from the men's department at some major retailer, certainly not Amish, but perhaps close enough from a distance if Brian was spying on them. He took off his broad-brimmed hat. "I didn't mean to interrupt."

"It's fine." Maryann tossed her gardening gloves aside and slipped out of the greenhouse past Zach. "I need to check on the girls. See that they're getting their chores done."

Heather watched Maryann leave, the fabric of her long dress swishing around her legs. She was sorry she had ruined the peaceful mood by her tactless questions about her mother's murder. Maryann had been her mother's dear friend.

Heather turned to Zach and noticed he was spinning the hat in his hands, a nervous gesture. Her heart plummeted. She sucked in a breath with eager anticipation. "Do you have news?"

SEVEN

"I don't have any news." Zach wished he did. He'd do anything to take away Heather's worry and see her smile. He blinked a few times, then stepped back, determined to maintain the wall of professionalism. He had a job to do. "Not concrete news, anyway," he clarified.

"What does that mean?" There was an edge to her voice as she turned away from him and shut off the hose in the greenhouse. She seemed to take her time rolling it up.

"Deputy Gates called me. They dragged the bottom of the creek and they haven't found Fox's body. The currents may have carried him out. Or maybe they didn't search the right spots. From the dock where he entered the boat to the point where we found the empty vessel was three-quarters of a mile."

"They may never find the body?" She crossed her arms and glared at him, as if somehow this was his fault.

"That's unlikely. But it might take a while. I'm sorry."

Heather bowed her head and ran a shaky hand across her hair, pushing back her bonnet. She took a moment to adjust her bonnet, then met his gaze. "What do I do now?" Her voice grew high-pitched. She waved her hand frantically up and down her Amish dress. The bonnet she had just adjusted. "Am I supposed to stay here? Hide forever?"

She spun around, paced a few steps, then turned back to him, shooting daggers at him with her steely gaze. She ripped off her bonnet and tossed it aside. It landed on the edge of a pot of mums in full bloom, dangled for a few seconds, then dropped to the floor of the greenhouse and settled into a puddle. He bent to pick it up, when she instructed him to leave it alone. With jerky movements, she yanked at the pins holding her hair in a neat bun at the base of her head. Her long brown hair cascaded over her shoulders in soft curls.

Combing her fingers frantically through her hair, she said, "I'm not going to spend another minute hiding." She drew in a ragged breath. "I wasted ten years already. Not to mention the years I had already wasted with Brian." She winced. "You said you shot him, right?" Her eyebrows rose as she waited for confirmation.

"Yes, I did."

"Then he's dead. I'm going to go back to living my life. Back to the bed-and-breakfast."

Doubt whispered across Zach's brain. His mind flashed back to the creek. To his erratic pulse pounding in his ears. Lifting his gun, aiming it at his target. He was a good shot. He *had* to have hit Fox.

Heather's life depended on it.

"Give it a few more days," Zach urged her. "They've extended the search north up the creek, cutting through the hills. If he lived long enough to get out near where the boat was found, he wouldn't have lived long. They'll find his body in the woods."

Her fingers edged with soil curled into a fist. "Then when his body doesn't turn up in the woods, you'll tell me to wait until they check north of there or west of here." Her face flushed red. "I have to believe he's dead. I'm done hiding."

Apparently sensing his apprehension, she stepped forward, looking like a woman straddling two worlds with her gorgeous long curls flowing down over her drab gray dress that only revealed the laces of her well-worn boots. She reached out and took his hat from his hands. A smile glinted in her eyes. "Now you don't have to pretend you're the Amish marshal."

Zach couldn't help but smile. "I thought I looked good in this hat."

She patted his chest. "You couldn't even commit to the entire ruse." She dropped her hand and adjusted the collar on his black golf shirt. "Now, *I* was committed."

He tipped his head and tried to read her. "It's not a good idea to go back to the bed-and-breakfast, you know."

"He's dead. I want to go back to my grand-mother's house on Lapp Road and get the bed-and-breakfast ready for our first guests." Heather bit her lower lip and her eyes grew glazed for a moment, as if she were trying to figure something out. "I've lost five days. I'm expecting guests in just over one week. It's time I go back."

Zach ran a hand over his mouth. "I can't—"

"You can't what?" Anger sparked in her eyes. "I let a man dictate what I wore, when I slept, what I *ate*! I am not going to let you tell me what to do."

Zach held up his hands in surrender. "Can I at least accompany you to the bed-and-break-fast? Stay a few more days. Until the body turns up."

"Your boss will let you stay longer?"

"He knows how important this case is to me." Besides, his boss owed him one for pulling him away from his vacation that he had planned to spend in his cabin surrounded by nothing but some dusty old books, a black-and-white TV and his feelings of guilt and self-recrimination.

Heather snagged the bonnet from the puddle on the floor and balled it up in her hand. "You're welcome to come to the bed-and-breakfast with me, but you know I'm going to put you to work."

"I wouldn't have it any other way."

A sense of pride filled Heather when Zach drove up to her grandmother's house. *Her* house now. They had used the unmarked vehicle the sheriff's department had left for their use until his truck was repaired. Ruthie had come along, insisting she needed to stay at the house to help with the preparations. Heather was happy for the company.

Looking at the house now was like seeing it for the first time. The workers had finished putting a fresh coat of gray paint on the shingled siding and the white trim gleamed anew.

For the briefest of moments she forget about all her troubles.

"Sloppy Sam did a great job," Ruthie said with a hint of pride she tried to suppress. The Amish were a humble people.

"Is there someplace I could park? In the barn maybe?" Zach asked.

Heather shot him a sideways look, knowing it was unreasonable to think these precautions weren't still necessary. "Sure. The barn's fine." She herself had decided to park her little car behind the barn because she still hadn't mustered the courage to go inside the barn. Maybe she never would.

As the truck bobbled over the ruts in the dirt driveway, she gasped in excitement when she saw the completed back of the house. "The window has been installed. Here—" she patted the dashboard "—let me out." She tugged on the door handle and climbed out of the truck, unable to take her eyes off the completed addition. The siding. The painting. The window. All complete.

Excitement bubbled up inside Heather as Ruthie jumped out and followed her. Heather dug into the bag she had strapped across her body and pulled out the house key. She ran up the back steps and unlocked the door. She pushed it open and the smell of new wood mingled with that of fresh paint. The kitchen was untouched, per Heather's request, except for the updated appliances. She wanted to feel her grandmother's presence. The workers had even seamlessly extended the wood floor from the kitchen into the new eating area.

"This is better than I imagined," Heather said. Sloppy Sam had built a long picnic table that could seat plenty of guests.

"Sloppy Sam is a craftsman," Ruthie said.

As Heather's gaze moved to the freshly painted wall to the right of the window, she found herself drawn forward. She ran her hand over the flat surface where the man who had tormented her for years had stood. Where he had scratched his creepy message. But thankfully, the workers had seen to it that no trace was left.

"Things will get better from here, I just know it," Ruthie said, smiling.

Heather smiled in return. Maybe, just maybe, she could finally allow herself to have hope again for the future.

She heard Zach at the back door. She squared her shoulders and met him in the kitchen. He had their bags slung over his shoulder.

Ruthie approached him and took her bag. "Heather, would you mind if I went upstairs to unpack?"

"Of course not. Go on." Heather had converted the smallest room upstairs—one too small for paying guests—to a cozy room for Ruthie, who initially intended to stay over only on weekend nights when the bed-and-breakfast had guests. The rest of the week, Ruthie would live at home and help with the greenhouse. And Heather had no plans to host guests during the week.

Zach placed the other bags on the floor in the new addition. "Place looks great."

"It does." She bit her lower lip, trying to contain her excitement. The silence stretched on for a beat too long. Heather took a step backward. "Let me show you where you can stay. There's a small space downstairs on the other side of the kitchen. It only has a cot, but…" She hadn't really thought this through.

"It'll be fine. Really." A smile twitched the corners of his mouth. "I'll put my bag away and be right back. You can give me a list of things you need done." He held out his hand. "But from the looks of it, this place is ready for visitors."

His smile was contagious. "I can always come up with a list."

"I didn't doubt that."

Heather strolled into the kitchen and braced her arms on the oversize kitchen sink. How often had her *mammy* stood in this very same spot, mourning the death of her daughter and the loss of her grandchildren? Heather wanted desperately to change the course of the future.

To find answers. To find happiness. And not to allow the ghost of Brian Fox to take that away from her.

"Okay, what's up first?"

She spun around and found Zach standing in the doorway with his arms crossed.

"Let me change, and then let's order a pizza for the three of us."

"Will they actually deliver way out here?"

Heather twisted her lips. "Oh, good point." She crossed the kitchen and opened the refrigerator, one of the few *Englisch* concessions to make running an "authentic" Amish bed-and-breakfast easier on her. Sure, she could have run a generator to all her kitchen appliances, but instead she had the contractor run electricity from the grid, definitely an Amish no-no, but her guests probably wouldn't think much of it. "I hadn't gone shopping yet, either. The few things Ruthie brought in the other day have rotted." For some reason, embarrassment heated her cheeks. Even after all these years, her response was instinctual. Brian would have yelled at her, called her an idiot, demanded his dinner. *Now!*

As her emotions welled and crested on a wave of panic, she reminded herself that the man standing a few feet away was not Brian. She swallowed back her emotions, closed the fridge door and turned to smile at him. "Any suggestions?"

"Absolutely. Let's go grocery shopping. I make a mean lasagna."

Zach laughed, apparently tickled by the surprise that must have registered in her eyes. "Don't you believe me?"

She held up her palms. "I have no reason not to. You've yet to disappoint me."

"I have no plans to."

Their eyes locked and lingered for a moment longer than was comfortable. Heather hadn't allowed herself to trust her feelings to another man after the havoc Brian wreaked on her life.

"Well—" Her voice cracked. "Give me ten minutes." She bent over and unlaced her muddy Amish boots and tossed them in the corner near the back door. Maybe she'd leave them there as part of the Amish decor. As she ran up the stairs of her new home, a sense of hope—real hope—for the future coursed through her.

Zach and Heather dropped Ruthie off to visit a friend while they went grocery shopping. It seemed Ruthie was excited to have a little freedom of her own. Her friend promised to hitch up her horse and bring Ruthie home sometime after dinner.

At the grocery store, Heather strolled ahead

of Zach. She had a lightness he'd never seen in her before. Up to this point, all of their contact—from the first time he met her at Jill's trial—had always been during stressful times. Now he sensed she was finally allowing herself to believe she was safe. He just hoped she was.

Next to the stand of bananas near the entryway, she spun around. "I'm not much of a cook, but I'm not sure this little store carries everything you'll need."

Zach leaned over and grabbed a shopping basket. "I'm sure we'll find everything we need."

They strolled companionably through the grocery store, picking up lettuce, tomatoes, noodles, sauce, cheese. He hadn't realized how hungry he was until he had all the ingredients for dinner in the basket.

Once they had purchased the groceries and arrived back home, he unloaded them onto the counter.

"Tell me what I can do," Heather said. "I may not know how to cook, but I can follow directions."

"Is that why you hired Ruthie? To cook?"

"In part. But mostly, I knew I couldn't run the bed-and-breakfast all on my own." The look in her eyes suggested something more.

Heather looked away and rubbed the back of

her neck. "Ruthie is going to stay here when I have guests. We've fixed up a cute little room for her upstairs. I'll pay her extra. I offered her room and board full-time, but I see now why she turned me down. Maryann and Emma still need her help at home."

"Yet the family needs the extra income."

Heather nodded her agreement.

Zach stopped breaking up the ground beef simmering in the pan on the stove and pointed toward the back door. "I'm going to make arrangements to have an alarm system installed."

Heather scratched her earlobe. "I can't afford that. I've spent everything I have on the remodel."

He watched her nervously tuck a strand of hair behind her ear while she pretended to be busy lining up the jar of sauce, ricotta cheese, and salt and pepper that he'd be needing shortly for the lasagna. His heart ached for her and he found himself drawn to her remarkable spirit.

"I'd like to install the alarm for you. A gift." He chopped up the ground beef with the edge of the spatula.

"Do you think I really need it?" Her soft tone sounded from just behind him.

He didn't turn around to answer. "I work in law enforcement. I've seen a lot of bad things in my career. You're out here in the middle of nowhere." He turned around, holding the spatula. A plop of ground beef hit the floor. They both squatted at the same time and bumped knees.

Heather laughed nervously and stood back up. "Here, let me get that." She tore a piece of paper towel from the roll, and from his crouched position he reached for the towel and she handed it to him. He wiped up the mess, straightened and tossed it in the garbage can.

Heather had gone pale as if a realization had washed over her. "You don't think Brian's dead, do you?"

He touched her arm. "I know I shot him. But it doesn't make any sense that they haven't found his body. However, even when we do have Fox back in custody or find out he's dead, it's not a smart idea for a young woman to live alone in a big house out in the country. You won't always have the benefit of houseguests." He pointed to the stairs. "We'll have a control panel installed in your bedroom."

She frowned at him as uncertainty flashed in her eyes.

"You're inviting strangers into your home. You need to take precautions."

A long-ago memory came to mind. His sister, Jill, had called him, panicked, frightened. She was afraid of her husband. By the time Jill met him at the door of her meticulously maintained home in the safe suburbs of Buffalo, she had changed her mind. Told her big brother that it was all a misunderstanding. Brian stood next to his baby sister, a smile on his face, his arm draped over her shoulders.

His possession.

Zach's gut roiled at the memory.

Nothing he'd said had convinced his sister to open up to him. To tell him what was really going on. To leave Fox. That day, Jill stood in the doorway with a fake smile on her face.

If only he had…

He shook his head, trying to dispel the horrible memory.

Heather slipped in beside him and stirred the beef that was spattering on the stove.

"Oh, I'm sorry." He covered her soft hand with his, taking the spatula from her. "Some cook I turned out to be."

Standing close, she smiled up at him. "If you think it's important that I get an alarm system, we'll do it. But I insist on paying you back." She searched his face.

"I do think it's important."

Heather gave him a quick nod. "I don't want you to stay here out of some misplaced sense of obligation."

"What do you mean?"

"You're not responsible for your sister's death."

Zach stopped stirring the beef on the stove. How had she read his mind?

"Brian is—*was*—a very convincing man," Heather said, her voice low. "He was charming. He persuaded me to stay more than once. Your sister was a beautiful, smart woman—" her words made the back of his throat ache "—and she was no more at fault for what happened to her than you were. Trust me, I've had my own share of guilt about your sister. What could I have done to prevent it? But I remind myself constantly that Brian is the only responsible party." She reached out and cupped his cheek, brushing her thumb across his jaw. He stood frozen, not wanting to feel too much. "You don't need to stay. I'll be okay." A soft hitch caught in her throat, as if she wasn't sure she believed her own words.

Zach took her hand and kissed the inside of her palm. "Do you want me to leave?"

She lowered her gaze, then lifted it again to meet his. "No, I don't want you to leave."

The tension eased out of his shoulders.

She reclaimed her hand and fisted it to her chest. "Not until we have proof Brian's dead."

EIGHT

Heather enjoyed the meal she and Zach—well, mostly Zach—had prepared. It was her first dinner in her *mammy*'s remodeled home. And it felt wonderful.

The sun lowered in the sky as they chatted over a frozen cake from Pepperidge Farm—apparently Zach drew the line at baking. She stood up from the new table and turned on the kerosene lamps, which created a soft glow. She sat back down next to Zach, not eager for the evening to be over.

"When are your first guests scheduled to arrive?"

"Next weekend." She moved the crumbs of the cake around on her plate. "Barring any cancellations. My plan is to only book rooms for the weekend."

"Well, hopefully this other issue will be resolved."

Heather studied the palm of her hand. "I

haven't watched any of the news coverage regarding the escape. I hope mention of an ongoing search for an escaped convict in Quail Hollow won't be bad for business."

Zach wiped his mouth with a napkin, then set it down, neatly running his fingers over the edge, creating a sharp fold.

"If I knew you better, I might think you were stalling," she said, trying to read his expression.

He drew in a deep breath. His dirty-blond hair looked darker in the heavy shadows. His eyes were hard to read. "The news mentioned that the search for Fox has focused on Quail Hollow because of you."

Heather's pulse whooshed in her ears as Zach's words seemed to be coming from miles away. "They mentioned me by name?" Of course they had. Hers was a juicy story. She swallowed hard. "Anything else?" She found herself holding her breath. "Did they mention my mother's murder?"

"Yes."

"How… Why?" But she knew why. Her mother's murder had been the only murder in the Amish community and now the next big story to hit the quiet town a generation later had a direct link: *her.* She groaned. "I wonder if this is going to ruin business." She snapped her gaze to him and laughed, rolling her eyes.

"No, no, it'll be great for business. Like how people like to take tours of morbid things, like Lizzie Borden's house or…" She dragged her hand through her hair. "Not that my mother died here. But her body…" She let the words trail off, not wanting to talk about it. Her mother's body had been found in the barn out back. *Her* barn. Another part of her past that she'd eventually have to face.

Zach covered her hand with his. "A news truck was out in front of your house a few days ago, but Deputy Gates chased it away. I don't think they gave him much of a fight because you weren't here. There's only so much coverage we can give to an empty house."

"But now that I'm back?"

"If they come back, we'll deal with it then. The truck's in the barn, so that should buy us more time."

"I suppose you're right. Why borrow trouble?" Heather leaned her shoulder against his. He shifted and wrapped his arm around her shoulders. "You saw the news coverage. What are they saying?"

She settled into his embrace and tuned into his comforting stroke on her arm. "It's not important."

Her eyes slowly closed. "I suppose you're right. It's not going to change anything." She suddenly bolted upright. His arm fell away from her and she angled her head to study him. "Did they put a photo of me on the news?"

"Heather…"

She recognized a stall when she heard it. "Tell me. Did they?"

"They ran coverage from when you testified. So yes."

She stood, suddenly very exhausted. "You're right, I shouldn't have asked. I was really hoping to live in anonymity. I guess that was too much to ask." Gathering the dishes, she carried them into the kitchen and over to the sink, wishing she could crawl into bed and sleep. Forget about her troubles for a few hours.

"Look on the bright side," Zach said, bringing a few more dishes over. "At least the Amish don't watch TV."

She narrowed her gaze at him skeptically. "I have a feeling news like this will make its way around Quail Hollow, TV or not. Ruthie seems to know things from town before I do." She shrugged as she filled up half the sink with hot soapy water. "This is where I need to rely on my faith. Trust God that things will work out."

He gently touched the small of her back. "Trust God and take precautions." She didn't miss the cynicism in his tone.

"I'll let the dishes soak and clean up in the

morning. It's early yet, but I'm tired." Maybe relaxing with a book would settle her nerves. She leaned forward and brushed a kiss across his cheek. "Good night, Zach. Thank you for everything." She took a step back. "You should find anything you need in the guest bathroom. If that fails, just give me a holler."

He nodded. "Night, Heather."

A current of electricity ran between them. He was here doing a job and then he'd be gone. Did she dare trust her heart to him only to be hurt again? Like Brian had hurt her.

Zach was nothing like Brian.

But how did she really know? How did anyone?

When she first met Brian, she would have never pegged him for the man he turned out to be.

Dismissing her swirling thoughts, she spun around and ran up the stairs. She slipped into her bedroom and shut the door and turned the dead bolt. She'd sleep better with the lock in place even with Zach downstairs.

Heather flopped down on the chaise lounge, her mind still racing. She hadn't had affectionate feelings toward a man since… She traced the stitching on the arm of the chair and drew in a deep breath. She could still smell the subtle scent of his aftershave. Feel the solidness of his arm around her.

She grabbed the blanket draped over the back of the chair and pulled it over her. Maybe she was confusing her feelings of security and protection for something more.

Something she thought she'd never have again.

She forgot about the book she planned to read and started to doze. She snapped to attention at the sound of footsteps on the stairs. Groggy from sleep, she stumbled toward the door, yet managed to keep her bare feet silent on the cold hardwood floor. Her fingers faltered at the knob to the dead bolt.

Mouth growing dry, she opened the door a fraction, relieved to see Ruthie passing in the hallway. "Good night," she whispered.

"Good night." The shadow of Ruthie's hand lifted in a quick wave. "See you in the morning."

Closing her door, Heather turned the bolt, relieved to know she was no longer alone.

The slant of sun cut across the edge of her bed, startling Heather awake. She bolted up, then stretched across and grabbed her cell phone to check the time.

After eight!

Throwing back the covers, she got cleaned up and dressed for the day and ran downstairs, both refreshed and embarrassed. She never slept this late *and* she still had a list of things to do. A week had passed since Heather had returned to the bed-and-breakfast with Zach and Ruthie in tow. The house had been abuzz with activity: Sloppy Sam and his crew finishing odd projects, Ruthie making lists and Zach helping out wherever he could. Everything seemed to be coming together.

And still no sign of Brian.

When Heather reached the kitchen, she found coffee already made in the coffeemaker—another one of her *Englisch* cheats—but no sign of Zach.

Unable to resist, she poured herself a cup, then sipped it while staring out the window over the yard. In just over twenty-four hours her first guests would be arriving. That was when she saw movement by the barn. Squinting, she noticed that it was Zach. He had found a wheelbarrow and a pitchfork and was hard at work.

"What are you doing, U.S. Marshal Zachary Walker?" she muttered to the empty kitchen, reminding herself that he was here because of his job. But even at that, he worked harder than one of Sloppy Sam's crew members. Zach knew the ins and outs of home repair. However, the longer he stayed, the harder it was to remind herself that he was here on business. Thankfully, Ruthie's presence kept Heather's emotions in check.

All of them had a job to do. *Period.*

Carefully holding her coffee so it wouldn't slosh out of the mug, Heather slipped her feet into her black Wellies and stepped outside. The sun beat down on the gorgeous fall day. She drew in a deep breath and some of the stress of the recent events washed off her.

She stood on the back stoop, sipping her coffee, hoping to get Zach's attention. After a few moments, he set aside the pitchfork and grabbed the handles of the wheelbarrow and pushed it out into the sun and directly toward her.

He stopped and set the wheelbarrow down and smiled. "Sleep well?"

"I did."

He squinted up at her and lifted a hand to tent his eyes. "I thought I'd put some hay down here so the guests wouldn't have to slop through the mud."

Heather smiled. "Good idea."

"What are your plans for the barn? It looks like it could use some TLC."

Heather's gaze drifted to the barn and her pulse automatically spiked. She had never stepped foot in the barn, nor did she have immediate plans to.

"Is something wrong?" The tone of Zach's voice suggested he had to repeat the question. Had he?

"Um…" She scratched the crown of her head and set her mug down on the top rail of the small porch. "I guess I never thought about it much." *That's a lie.* The barn hunkered on the property like a beast ready to get up and strike.

"If I patched up the roof, it would prevent more rain damage. I'm sure tourists would love to go into a barn and explore, but in its current condition, it's a little dangerous."

"I'm out of funds for now," she said curtly, walking down to the wheelbarrow and grabbing a fistful of hay. She shook it out over the muddy path.

As Heather reached for more, Zach touched her wrist, stopping her mid motion. "Is there something you're not telling me?"

She sprinkled the hay over the mud, then brushed her palms together. She tucked her hands under her armpits as a sudden chill raced up her spine. "They found my mother's body in the barn."

Zach seemed to reel back. "Oh, I had no idea. I'm sorry. I shouldn't have pushed."

She shook her head. "No, it's okay. Part of

the reason I came here was to face my past."
Her tone was droll. "I had no idea I'd be facing
so much of my past all at once."

"The offer still stands. I could patch the
roof."

She scratched her neck. "Let me think about
it."

"Okay." He turned and got to the business of
spreading the hay.

Ruthie rounded the corner of the house
and stopped. "*Gut* morning," she sang good-
naturedly. "I see you're finally up."

"Good morning." Heather smiled. "Yes, I
was tired."

Ruthie brushed her hands together. "I planted
some flowers by the mailbox out front. Sloppy
Sam ran me home to pick some up from the
greenhouse."

"Thank you. That's a nice touch."

"Did you still want to go to the grocery store
this morning?" Ruthie asked.

Heather picked up her coffee mug from the
rail and opened the back door, allowing Ruthie
to go in first. "Yes. Let's finish our list first."

Before disappearing inside, she turned to
Zach. "If you promise not to fall off the roof
and break your neck, I think it would be great
to patch the holes in the barn." She didn't need
a liability on her property.

Heather could feel Ruthie's gaze on her. Most locals knew the story of her mom's murder even though it had happened before the young Amish woman's time. "I thought—"

"Perhaps someday I'd like to own horses. Maybe get a buggy. Do Amish tours." Heather smiled. "Lots of potential."

Zach covered his heart and gave her a solemn look. "Promise I won't fall through the roof."

"Please don't. That's the last thing I need." She shot him a pointed glare. "Be careful. I'm going inside. Ruthie and I need to make our grocery list."

"Do you need a ride?"

"No, my car is parked behind the barn. Hold on." She scooted into the house, grabbed the set of keys from the hook and returned, tossing them to Zach. He caught them in one hand. "Can you pull it around for us?"

A worry whispered across her brain. She prayed Brian hadn't taken his frustration out on her car as he had done on Zach's. She had gotten so spoiled this past week being driven around by Zach first in his loaned vehicle and now his repaired one, she hadn't given her car much thought. It wasn't much of a car, but at this point, she couldn't afford to replace it.

"Sure thing. I'll bring it around to the driveway."

Ruthie and Heather watched him jog to the backside of the barn. "Isn't he helpful?" Ruthie asked playfully.

"Yes, yes, he is."

Despite Heather's protest, Zach decided he should escort her and Ruthie to the grocery store. He was relieved to find her car had remained untouched. Maybe Fox hadn't noticed it parked behind the barn.

Once Ruthie and Heather were safely home and inside, creating a menu for the guests, Zach decided today would be a good day to inspect the damage to the barn. When his parents first got the cabin in the woods some ten years ago, Zach had done many of the repairs and updates. It had been a therapy of sorts.

He found a ladder in the yard and propped it against the side and climbed up and inspected the roof. With some plywood and shingles, he could make this thing as good as new. Well, at least it would be a start. The way it was now, rain would continue to damage the structure to the point of no return. *Maybe Heather would prefer that.*

Zach made a few mental notes, then climbed down the ladder. Far from the house so nobody would overhear, he decided to give Deputy Gates a call and ask him about Sarah Miller's murder. Gates seemed more than eager to discuss the case that had marred his father's tenure as sheriff.

"There had been a vagrant passing through town at the time of Mrs. Miller's disappearance. A middle-aged man who seemed to be homeless and acting strange. Might have had mental health issues. Anyway, he left town at the same time Sarah Miller went missing."

"Did anyone see Sarah with the man?"

"Not per se. But Sarah had been in town one of the days the man was begging for food outside the grocery store. Her children remembered that she gave him food. The Amish are kind that way."

"And you think maybe he became fixated on Sarah because of this?" Zach let out a long breath. Unstable people had become obsessed with their victims over far less.

"That was our best guess. But even with a sketch of the suspect widely distributed, no one identified the guy. Case grew cold." The deputy cleared his throat. "Now it's what, twenty-some years later? You're not thinking about digging into this case, are you?"

Zach turned and looked at the house. No one had come outside. "I guess the law enforcement side of me made me curious."

"Oh, plenty of people have been curious, but

the case has gone unsolved. I'm afraid it'll always be that way. It was a dark page in the quiet town's history. My poor father, despite being retired, still brings up that case now and again."

"Sarah Miller's body was found in the barn behind the Lapp property?"

"Yeah…" Zach shifted his stance and hooked his thumbs into his belt. "Hard to say if her body had been there all along or if the murderer had dumped it there just prior to her being found."

"Didn't the Millers use the barn?"

"Sure did. But Sarah's horse had gone missing, too. No reason to go into the stall without the horse."

"Did they ever find the horse?"

"Yes, about a week later. An Amish farmer from the next district over brought it around once word reached him about Sarah's disappearance."

Zach rubbed his jaw. "Thanks for the information."

Ending the call, Zach walked around to the front of the barn and entered it again, this time with a new awareness. It wasn't a large barn, so the fact that her body had remained missing for a few days meant that it had either been moved or hidden.

A little voice deep in his head scolded him

for not just enjoying this fall day. And instead of appreciating the lull in the case against Fox and salvaging part of his vacation, he was mentally digging into a cold case.

Totally not his job.

But finding answers was important to Heather, so it had become important to him. He inspected the entire barn. Sun streamed in through the broken slats and dust particles floated in the air. A ladder was propped up against the loft. He hadn't remembered seeing the ladder there the night they searched the barn for Fox. Perhaps one of the workmen had brought it in more recently. He grabbed a rung and shook it. Seemed sturdy enough.

Carefully checking each ladder rung as he climbed, he reached the top and stepped into the loft. The strong sent of dried wood reached his nose. He crossed to the wall and slid open the loft door. He held on to the frame, realizing that though the drop to the grass below might not kill him, it wouldn't feel good.

And he had promised Heather he wouldn't break his neck.

From here, he had an unobstructed view across the yard to the upstairs bedrooms at the back of the house, including Heather's. Someone could sit here and watch.

A chill skittered down his spine. He pulled

his cell phone out of his back pocket and turned
on the flashlight. He shined it around the loft
and stopped when he found a fast-food restaurant bag crumpled up. He picked it up and
carried it over to the light by the opening. Un-
folding the bag slowly, he smelled the not-too-
old scent of French fries.

Strange.

He rooted around the bag and found a receipt. He pulled it out and stared at it, blinking rapidly. It was dated yesterday afternoon.

NINE

Deputy Gates left with the fast-food garbage and the assurances that it was probably just some local kids taking advantage of an abandoned barn. Sloppy Sam and his crew, once contacted, assured the deputy that they all brought lunches from home. Just to cover all their bases, the deputy promised to check if the restaurant had any video of the person making the purchase at the time stamped on the receipt.

Heather turned to Zach. "Do you think it's something more?"

Zach crossed his arms over his solid chest and sighed, which was far more telling than any words. "I thought it was important enough to call the sheriff's department."

Ruthie sat rocking in one of the chairs next to the wood-burning stove. "Kids go up into barn lofts all the time. Even Amish kids. It's a perfect place to party. No one can see you from the road."

"But it was just one bag. If it was a party, wouldn't there be discarded beer bottles? More garbage? Not just one fast-food bag."

Zach touched her wrist. "We have no reason to think it was Fox."

Heather lifted an eyebrow at the mention of her ex-husband's name. Of course she had been thinking it was Brian, but to hear Zach give voice to her suspicions made the fine hair on the back of her neck stand on edge. She cleared her throat. "Are we safe here?"

"I'll make sure you're safe. We have an alarm system now, too." The workers had installed it a few days ago. The modern technology may have detracted from the Amish vibe, but Heather had already felt safer at night when the alarm was activated.

Ruthie pushed to her feet. "Everything will be fine. And we can't let down our first guests tomorrow."

Heather nodded. "I suppose you're right. Oh, wait…" She hustled into the kitchen and came back with a slip of paper. "I almost forgot with all this craziness going on. I got a last-minute reservation. A young woman wanted a place to stay as a writing retreat. Something about a book deadline and she was looking for some quiet." She laughed nervously. "I hope I can provide the quiet she needs. Either that or fodder for her next story."

"Don't think like that. This is great. We have a full house," Ruthie said.

"Yes." Heather was afraid to allow the spark of hope flickering in her belly to burn bright.

"Let's continue with our plans as scheduled and not allow some garbage in the barn to throw us off course. Like Ruthie said, it was probably some kids." Zach gently brushed his hand down Heather's arm.

"I talked to my boss right after the incident here," Zach added. "He's going to put a call out and have a search party fan out from the barn. Can't hurt."

"But…" Heather stopped herself. She didn't want to sound like a petulant child whining that she thought Brian was supposed to be dead, not having fast food in her barn.

"It's a precaution. That's all. They're not going to allow anything to happen to you. *I'm* not going to allow anything to happen to you."

Ruthie gestured with her bonneted head toward the stairs. "Let's get the pink room ready. It has a nice chair and a desk. I'm sure our newest guest will love it. The afternoon light in the room is great, I mean if she's going to be in there writing a book." Ruthie drew up her shoulders and smiled brightly, as if work was a treat. "Isn't this exciting?"

Heather followed Ruthie upstairs. Her young employee's enthusiasm was contagious.

Zach couldn't sleep much, so he found himself patrolling the property, checking all the outbuildings, including the loft of the barn. The only thing that kept him company outside was the chill and the crickets.

There was absolutely no sign of anyone.

The stillness brought a certain peace to Zach, a man who was otherwise always on an assignment or surrounded by the buzz of his hometown. He enjoyed a certain energy from that, but stillness was good, too.

He made his way around the property once again, but this time he slowed by the barn and turned around and stared up at the house. The way the land rose to meet the barn, it gave a clear view of the house. Once again, he wondered if Brian had watched the house—watched Heather—while snacking on French fries and a burger.

Zach's phone dinged and he glanced down. A new email had come in. Out of habit, he tapped through and opened it, surprised, or maybe not, that his boss was still awake at this hour and sending emails.

As he read, his stomach dropped. The sheriff's department hadn't found anything suspicious on the fast-food restaurant's video feed. The local high school basketball team and the requisite cheerleaders had gone in around that time for an after-school celebration. No sign of Fox. And since all indications were that Fox had perished, it was time for Zach to report back to the office. The U.S. Marshals office had other cases that now required his attention.

Frustration heated his cheeks. He was *not* going to leave Heather. Not yet. Something in his gut told him this case wasn't settled, the most obvious sign being that they hadn't found Fox's body. But it had been over a week. Where was it?

A little voice whispered in Zach's head. *Not going to leave here because you think her life is in danger or because you don't want to leave her?*

He honestly didn't know the answer. Perhaps a little of both. Less of the first, more of the second. At least that was what he wanted to believe. He wanted Heather to be able to live out her dream in peace.

It was after midnight. His boss was obviously up. Zach tapped the phone's screen and lifted it to his ear.

"Don't you ever sleep?" Kenner said by way of greeting.

"I could say the same thing." Zach ran a hand over his hair. He could use a trim. He liked to keep it military short.

"You got the email?"

"Yeah. What case do you need me back for?"

"A few. You know how it is. The caseload on your desk isn't getting any smaller."

"But—" he turned his back to the house, not that anyone was awake and in earshot "—I had vacation I didn't use when Fox escaped."

"I know." His tone suggested he wasn't going to give Zach any slack because of it. "But it's been a couple weeks. We need you back in the office."

"What if I told you I wasn't ready to come back? I need to stay to see this thing through."

"We both know Fox can't still be out in the woods."

"I'm not going to feel Heather is safe until I see his body."

"Heather, huh? I know how personal this case is," he said, his tone a mix of sympathy and understanding. "But perhaps you've made it even more personal."

Zach bit his tongue. Understanding he appreciated, sympathy not so much. The soft lilt of sympathy suggested that his boss thought he wasn't thinking clearly. That he had allowed his personal feelings to cloud his professional judgment.

"We both know this could drag on for weeks, months… It may never be resolved," his boss said.

Zach groaned. The thought of no closure twisted his gut. He needed to know Fox was dead. Then he could go back to his life knowing the man who had killed his sister wasn't roaming free.

"We've worked together for a long time. We've been friends for a long time," Kenner added. "Don't do this to yourself. Come back to the office. We'll get you busy on another case."

"Can I give you my answer tomorrow? I'm not sure I'm ready to come home."

A long, tension-filled pause extended across the line. Finally his boss spoke. "I'll give you till Monday morning. But I want your answer then."

"And if I don't come back?"

"I'm not going to lie. We need you here, and if you defy a direct order, it will affect your career."

"I'll take my chances." Zach pressed End and slid the phone back into his pocket.

A twig snapped behind him and he spun around as he reached for his gun.

Heather's hands came up and her wide eyes glistened in the moonlight. "It's me. It's me."

Zach's heart was up in his throat. "Haven't you ever heard you're not supposed to sneak up on a guy who has a gun?"

"I didn't want to interrupt your phone call." A hint of annoyance edged her tone. "Was that work?"

"Yeah." He started walking toward the house, not comfortable with having Heather out here in the open in the middle of the night. "Come on." He touched the small of her back.

Heather glanced up at him as they walked toward the house. "Yeah, it was work. But it's nothing for you to worry about."

"Please don't do that to me. I'm not a little delicate flower."

Shame heated his cheeks. "I'm sorry. My boss got info back on the video at the fast-food restaurant. Nothing indicates Fox purchased the food at the time on the receipt found in the loft."

"That's good, right?" She tilted her head, but he didn't want to meet her gaze. "Dead men don't get hungry, right?"

He couldn't help but smile. "No, they don't."

"Does this mean you're leaving?"

She must have overheard his conversation.

"I have to decide by Monday."

Heather held out her hands, indicating the house and the land surrounding them. "I think we have everything under control. I can't ask you to stay, even though the barn roof ain't gonna fix itself."

Zach laughed. "Yeah, maybe it is time to go home."

Heather ran the dust rag over the oak of the rockers, more for something to do than out of necessity. The house was ready. *More* than ready.

A mixture of excitement and a touch of disappointment ran through her. Today was opening day. The fruit of all their labor. Yet she couldn't shake the feelings of loss that had lingered with her as she drifted off to sleep and then again when she woke up.

Zach was leaving on Monday.

In the short time she had spent with Zach, she had grown to really like him, but now with him going back to Buffalo, they wouldn't be able to explore what might have been.

She flipped the rag around to find a clean spot and ran it over the windowsills. Maybe it was just as well. She didn't need the added complication of a man.

Footsteps sounded on the hardwood floor and Heather's heart leaped in her throat. She spun around to find Ruthie on the stairs. Heather tried to hide the disappointment she felt in her heart.

Ruthie must have witnessed it, because she made a dramatic show of pressing her hand to her heart. "I'm happy to see you, too, Miss Miller."

Heat fired in Heather's cheeks. "No, um... you surprised me. Good morning." She tucked the dust rag into her back pocket and smiled. "Ready for our first big day?"

"Yah." A hint of Pennsylvania Dutch slipped in. "We'll serve a light snack around seven this evening. Most of the guests will have eaten before they check in."

"Yes, that's the plan." Heather crossed the room and palmed the banister. "I appreciate all your help. I wouldn't be able to do this on my own."

A shuffling drew her attention to the kitchen. Zach stared at her with a funny expression on his face. She wondered if he had made a firm decision to leave on Monday.

Of course he had. He couldn't stay here forever.

"Anything specific you need me to do today?"

Heather clasped her hands together. "I think we're set."

* * *

Mr. and Mrs. Hopkins and Mr. and Mrs. Woodruff sat around the table and chitchatted, seeming like they were more interested in talking about who they knew in common in Buffalo than they were about talking to the real live Amish person walking in and out of the room serving shoofly pie and tea and coffee.

Heather suspected the guests had also discussed the search for the ex-convict who had made his way to Quail Hollow, but either out of consideration or maybe just by chance, she hadn't heard anything as of yet. She hoped it remained that way. She hated to be the focus of gossip.

Miss Fiona Lavocat, their last-minute guest, hadn't arrived yet. Heather pulled back the front curtain and a whisper of worry sent goose bumps across her skin. It seemed late for a single woman to be traveling alone.

Dropping the curtain back into place, Heather forced herself to relax her shoulders. She was probably projecting her own feelings. That was what happened when you spent the majority of your adulthood hiding from an abusive ex-husband.

She smiled politely at her guests as she slipped past the dining area and into the kitchen. She turned on the tap and filled the sink with hot soapy water. Something about washing dishes by hand was therapeutic. Beyond her kitchen window, as she swished the inside of a tall glass with a sponge on a plastic stick, she saw Zach unloading some plywood from the back of his pickup truck. His vehicle provided the only light in the gathering dusk. She didn't want to read too much into the delivery. Was he going to be around long enough to finish the job? He didn't strike her as the kind of guy who didn't finish what he started.

Maybe he was just picking up some supplies for Sloppy Sam.

A knocking sounded on the front door. Heather set the glass in the drying rack, wiped her hands on a dishrag and hustled toward the door. She waved to Ruthie, who was collecting dishes from the table. "I'll get it." She'd much rather Ruthie entertain the guests.

Through the glass on the top half of the door, she noticed a young woman with long red hair falling over her shoulders. She seemed to be looking everywhere but through the window at Heather. She pulled open the door. "You must be Fiona."

The young woman adjusted her glasses and smiled. "I am. I had trouble finding the bed-and-breakfast." She hiked up the strap of her bag and bent her knees slightly to reach for the handle of her suitcase.

"Let me get that." Heather stepped onto the porch and reached for the bag.

"I've got it." Fiona lifted the bag into the house and set it down on the hardwood floor. She took in the room. "Wow, this is a real Amish house?"

Something about the way she said it made Heather bristle. She just hoped she was able to hide her reaction. Isn't this what she had wanted guests to think? Yet a little piece of her felt like she was trading on her family's past for profit.

Heather swallowed and forced a smile. "My *mammy* was Amish. This was her house." Her "go-to" had always been to say her grandmother was Amish, but what about her *mem*? What about her? However, truth be told, she had never been baptized—the Amish waited for adulthood—so although she had lived as the Amish until she turned six, she hadn't been fully brought into the faith.

She cleared her throat, wishing she could stop her rambling thoughts.

Fiona dropped her laptop bag by the door next to her suitcase and strolled around the room. "This is so cool." Then she stopped and turned around and made a strange I-should-have-thought-to-ask-this-before face. "I'm going to need to charge my laptop. Will that be a problem?"

"No, not at all. When I had the renovations done, I added a few modern conveniences. You'll find an outlet in your bedroom as well as one in the bathroom."

"Good, good." Fiona placed her hands on her hips. "I should get a lot of work done here out in the middle of nowhere."

"How did you find us?"

"Your website. I googled B and Bs in Western New York. There were so many. There are a ton in Niagara Falls, but I wanted to find somewhere less…busy, I guess. Less temptation to go out and visit a wax museum or something." A grimace flashed across her face as if she had said something wrong. "Am I supposed to check in or something?"

Heather shook her head, feeling a little foolish. She figured she'd get into a rhythm soon enough. She slid up the cover on the rolltop desk, opened a notebook and entered Fiona's name. She had decided paper and pens would seem more quaint. However, she had the ability to run a credit card through her smartphone. Fiona reached into her bag and pulled out a roll of bills. "Is cash okay?" She shrugged, a sheepish expression on her face. "I don't have a credit card."

"Yes, cash is fine."

Laughter rose from the eating area. Even though the two couples had just met, it seemed they had really hit it off. Fiona glanced in that direction with mild disinterest. "Busy weekend."

Heather held up her hand. "You'll have your own bedroom. Ruthie picked out a nice room with a cozy chair and a desk. I'm sure it'll be very quiet. You can listen to the corn grow." Heather sometimes wished she could make herself stop talking.

"Sounds great." Fiona reached for her laptop case.

"Um, I do need ID. Do you have a driver's license? It's just a formality." Heather wasn't sure why she felt silly for asking this young woman for ID. She was running a business. It wasn't a paranoid thing to do.

Fiona seemed to flinch. "Oh, of course." She slid her fingers into a narrow compartment on her laptop case and pulled out a New York State driver's license. "I parked on the edge of the driveway behind the other cars. Is that okay?"

"Yes. That's fine."

As Heather jotted down Fiona's information so she could track the woman down if, say, she damaged her room, Fiona leaned in close and whispered, "I almost didn't book this bed-and-breakfast when I realized this was in the same town where they're looking for that escaped convict."

Heather froze, pen poised above the piece of paper. She slowly lifted her eyes to meet Fiona's. "Well, I'm glad you didn't cancel." Heather prayed that her expression didn't give away the emotions rioting inside her.

"Should I be worried?" The two women locked gazes a moment and Heather tried to decipher in that one look if Fiona knew of her personal ties to the missing convict.

"No, not at all." Heather noticed Zach enter the front door at that exact moment. "There's no need to worry. Law enforcement has combed this area, and if Brian Fox was in Quail Hollow, he's long gone by now."

A small frown tipped the corners of Fiona's mouth. The expression on her face shifted from mild curiosity to one of expectation as she stood clutching her bags.

"I'll show you to your room," Heather said, snapping the register closed and sliding the roll-top desk down.

"I'll show her to the room." Ruthie's voice startled Heather. The young Amish woman had entered the living room from the other direction just as quietly as Zach had, either that or Heather had just been a little jumpy.

"Thank you." Heather held out her palm to Ruthie. "This is Ruthie. Ruthie, this is our guest Miss Lavocat."

"Oh, please, it's Fiona."

"Okay, Fiona. Ruthie'll show you to your room."

Fiona lifted her shoulders, then let them drop. "Sounds good."

"I'll take your bag," Zach offered.

Ruthie slipped in and grabbed it. "No need. I've got it."

Heather sensed Zach watching her, but oddly it didn't unnerve her. She turned to him and smiled. "You've been working hard."

"I believe I've run out of daylight." He brushed his hands on the thighs of his jeans. "How do you contact your Amish contractor? Does he have a phone?"

"Yes." She feared the brightness of her smile wavered. Zach wanted to hand off the work. Did this mean he was leaving? "I have his number in my desk."

She took a step toward the desk and Zach said, "It can wait till tomorrow."

"Okay. I guess I should see if our guests need anything else."

Heather noticed that Ruthie had already

cleared the table. Upon seeing her, the guests looked up expectantly. "You have a very nice home," Mrs. Woodruff said.

"Thank you. Can I get you anything else?"

They all said they were fine, so Heather excused herself and went upstairs, fully intending to come back down after her guests had settled in for the night and make sure the last few coffee mugs were cleared away and all the doors were locked. A niggling that she had forgotten something wouldn't leave her. Soon, she'd get into a routine, but she had to give herself some slack. This was, after all, her first night with guests in her bed-and-breakfast.

Zach had retreated to his room a few minutes earlier. From the upstairs landing, Heather could hear Ruthie talking to Fiona. She slipped into her room and wished she could have just crawled into bed and called it a night. Her eyes felt gritty and a headache threatened. She figured she better take something for it because she couldn't afford any downtime with guests in her home.

She opened her medicine cabinet and sucked in a gasp. Panic sliced through her as she reached in with a shaky hand and picked up a simple gold wedding band. With narrowing vision, she read the inscription:

Forever Mine.

Followed by the date of her wedding to Brian Fox.

The ring slipped out of her grasp and bounced around the bowl of the sink. She clamped her hand over it before it slipped down the drain. She scooped it up with her fingers and set it back on the shelf where she had found it and stared at it as the walls closed in on her.

TEN

Zach stood by the window and stared out over the farmland. He had enjoyed the hard labor today. It felt good to get out of his head for a bit. His boss was telling him he was needed at the office. But too much was left undone here.

They still hadn't found Fox's body.

A quiet knock sounded on his door and he frowned and turned around. He crossed the small room to the door and found a pale Heather standing in his doorway under the soft glow of the kitchen light. Behind her in the eating nook, the guests' good-humored conversation indicated they were oblivious to whatever had brought Heather to his door. She was shaking.

"What is it? Is everything okay?" He looked past her, half expecting Fox to be standing behind her. He blinked and the image disappeared.

Heather lifted a shaky hand and tucked a

strand of hair behind her ear. "I have to show you something." Her voice trembled.

"Okay." He searched her eyes, but she seemed to be a million miles away.

As they walked past the guests, Heather smiled and said, "The upstairs faucet seems to be dripping in my bathroom."

Zach followed her upstairs and the door down the hall opened and Fiona peeked out, gripping her bathrobe closed at the collar. "Oh, I'm sorry. I heard voices and I wondered. I didn't mean to—"

"Everything's okay," Zach said. "Miss Miller has been having issues with the faucet."

"Okay. Well, good night, then." The young woman closed the door with a quiet click, leaving Heather and Zach in the hallway alone.

"Come on. Show me what has you so rattled," he said.

Zach followed Heather through her suite into her private bathroom. She stood with her arms crossed staring at the mirror, but not at her image reflected in it. "What is it?"

She pointed at the mirror. "Look in the medicine cabinet."

He pulled on one side of the mirror, then the other before he heard a quiet click and the latch released, revealing the medicine cabinet behind the mirror. A single bottle of pain reliever sat inside next to a simple gold wedding ring. He turned and looked at Heather. She had that glassy look again. He saw her visibly swallow. "The ring. Read the inscription," she whispered.

Zach stared at her for a minute longer before picking up the ring and turning it so he could read the inscription. Dread knotted his stomach as he realized the significance of it. "Your wedding ring?"

Her hand fluttered around the hollow of her throat. "Yes." The word came out on a single breath. "He was here."

He cupped Heather's elbow and felt a slight tremble race through her. "When was the last time you went into the medicine cabinet?"

She blinked slowly, as if thinking. "I put the pain reliever in there when I moved in, but haven't opened the door since."

"When did you last see this ring?" He ushered her out of the bathroom and she sat on the edge of the chaise lounge while Zach paced the space in front of her.

"I left it behind when I ran away."

"You left it at the home you shared with Fox?"

She nodded and dragged a shaky hand across her hair. "I took it off and set it on the kitchen table. I wanted him to know I had left him. It was an act of defiance just before I took the biggest risk of my life." She lifted her watery gaze to him. "He was in my room. He's not dead."

Zach stopped pacing and crouched down in front of her and gathered her hands in his. "This doesn't mean that he's alive. He may have made his way up here the night he left the message on the back wall for you. He may have slipped upstairs, then escaped out the front door while we were by the back door. Any number of possibilities that don't include a return trip to your house."

Heather pressed her hands to her mouth. "How do we know for sure?"

He didn't.

"His body has to be recovered." It wasn't fair that Heather had to live with this doubt. Zach stood and gently brushed the back of his knuckles across her warm cheek. "I'm not going anywhere until then."

Heather nodded, but uncertainty flashed in the depths of her eyes. "Your boss..." They both knew that finding Fox's body wasn't a certainty. Zach couldn't stay here forever.

"My boss is going to have to understand."

"But..." Heather tried to argue.

"I need to make sure you're safe." He cleared his throat. "Now, about this ring. You were still married when you left Fox?"

"Yes. I had to leave him. If I didn't, he would have—" The word *killed* died on her lips. "I'm sorry."

"Don't be. How did you arrange a divorce?"

"I didn't for a long time. I had to stay hidden. But when Brian met Jill, he wanted a divorce and reached out to me through my sister. It was through her that I communicated with a lawyer and the divorce was finalized." She frowned. "I moved again after that. I couldn't risk him coming for me. No one disobeyed Brian and got away unscathed."

"No." No, they didn't. He had killed Jill the day after she called her big brother begging for a way out. He'd been out of town on a case. He'd told her to leave the house that night. To go to his apartment and lock herself in. Brian had found her. Slaughtered her on the back steps. Her favorite purple suitcase dumped on top of her lifeless body.

Heather untucked her legs and stood, sighing heavily. "I'm tired. I need to go to sleep."

"Of course." He smiled and backed out of the room, slipping out of the door that had been left ajar. He paused just outside the doorway thinking he heard footsteps somewhere on the second floor. All the rooms were occupied by guests and the hall was empty. It was now quiet downstairs.

Just to be safe, he double-checked the doors and windows throughout the house and then returned to his room on the first floor. With various guests in the house, it would be difficult to assure that all the doors and windows remained locked without scaring the guests. Nor could he set the alarm in case a guest wanted to go outside.

Why are you so worried? Dead men don't crawl through windows.

The ring had set off new concerns. Had Fox left it on his first visit? Or had he somehow returned?

Zach sat down on the edge of the cot. Until there was a body—definitive proof of Fox's death—Zach would remain vigilant even if it meant sleeping with one eye open.

With a bowl of fruit in her hands, Heather froze on the other side of the entry to the addition, where her guests had gathered. Fiona was holding court, her voice a hushed whisper.

"Brian Fox, the convict running loose in Western New York, had been married to Heather Miller."

"What?" one of the older gentleman said, either in disbelief or because he was hard of hearing.

"Yeah, she testified against Brian after he

killed his second wife." Fiona relayed the information as if she was doling out juicy gossip on the middle school playground. Anger swirled in Heather's gut as this stranger violated her privacy. Why hadn't Fiona mentioned any of this to her last night when they chatted? Instead she acted as if she barely knew about "that escaped convict."

Heather had been so used to being tucked away, she'd never get comfortable with having the details of her life splayed out for all to see.

"You okay?"

Heather spun around and bumped into Ruthie with the edge of the bowl. "Can you put this on the table? I think they have everything they need for breakfast. I have to do something."

Ruthie took the bowl with a smile. Heather drew in a deep breath and opened the back door and stepped outside. The cool autumn air hit her fiery cheeks.

Her gaze drifted to the barn, where Zach was already setting up work for the day. She crossed the yard to him, her mood immediately lifting. He looked up from where he had a piece of wood balanced on a table.

"You really don't have to do all this." Heather tented a hand over her eyes and looked up at the barn.

"I enjoy it."

"I appreciate it." She stared at the small pile of sawdust on the hard-packed earth. "And thanks for being there last night. I don't know what I would have done. That ring really rattled me. You really think he left it the night he broke into my house?"

"I called in the information to my boss. He'll see that the proper authorities know of the development. But yes, I don't think Fox came back to the house. Even if he had survived, it would have been too risky."

"You don't know Brian like I do. He's not rational."

"Once we find him, you won't have to worry about him ever again." His gaze drifted to the back of the house, then to her. "My boss gave me another week."

"Because of the ring?"

"Yes."

A puddle of conflicting emotions pooled in her belly. She was relieved Zach was staying, but concerned that his reassurances regarding the ring were merely lip service. But what could he tell her that she hadn't already considered?

"I'm glad you're staying," she finally said. "I'd feel better if we had more answers."

"Me, too." He picked up a piece of wood

and placed it flat on the workbench. "I figured you'd be occupied for a while with breakfast."

"Ruthie and I already set up the breakfast buffet. I had to get out for a bit." She crossed her arms and rocked back on her heels. "Fiona, our young writer, decided it would be fun to tell the other guests that I'm the infamous Brian Fox's ex-wife." Another wave of pinpricks washed over her. "As much as I hated hiding from Brian, I enjoyed the anonymity of it. I hate being the subject of gossip. It's so intrusive. And I can't imagine it'll be good for business."

Zach rested his palms on the plywood and squinted at the house. "Things will quiet down eventually." He drew in a deep breath. "You'll never be able to let it go completely, but the people around you will stop talking about it as they move on to the next drama."

"Mmm…" Heather feared things would never quiet down. That she'd never be able to face the past. *All of her past.*

She took a step toward the barn and her knees grew weak. "I haven't been in the barn since I learned that that's where they found my mother's body." A band of dread tightened around her chest and made her dizzy.

She touched the door frame, waiting, for what she wasn't sure. The scent of damp hay and aging wood reached her nose. A surreal feeling made the old wooden walls heave and sway.

Her father had said her mother had loved her horse and probably would have become a veterinarian if there were such a thing among the Amish. But generally the Amish only went to school through the eighth grade.

A person didn't need an education to live the Amish way.

Heather stepped into the barn and slowly walked toward the stalls where her mother's body had been found. She wasn't sure which one. One of the planks of wood along the back wall had rotted away due to dampness and age.

She turned when she felt Zach's hand on her shoulder. "I thought I'd feel something more knowing this was where my mother was found."

"I'm so sorry."

Heather turned away from the stalls. "The local sheriff was convinced it was a random person traveling through town. My father never wanted to talk about it, but he finally said that any leads never panned out. My dad said I had to forgive the man who killed my mother. That's the Amish way. My father had given up everything Amish, but he clung to that. Forgiveness. I think it's what allowed him to keep going." She dragged a hand through her hair. "I haven't been able to find forgiveness."

"You've had to deal with more tragedy in your, what—" He lifted his eyebrows.

"Thirty-two years." She smiled at his round-about way of asking how old she was, not that it mattered.

"Yes, most people haven't had to go through what you've had to deal with in their entire lifetime."

"I'm not looking for sympathy. God has blessed me in more ways than I can count." She turned and stepped outside of the barn, letting the sun warm her goose-pimpled skin.

"How do you do that?"

Heather turned to look at Zach standing next to her. "How do I do what?"

"Have faith despite everything that has happened to you?"

Heather opened her mouth to say something, then thought better of it, considering his sister was dead.

"Tell me, what were you about to say?"

Heather met his gaze squarely. "I was going to say that I'm blessed to still be alive. To see the sunrise. To feel the cool air on my skin. But then I realized how trite that would sound to someone who had lost someone to murder. I imagine your sister also had faith."

"She did."

"Yet, despite her faith, evil found her. So I understand why your faith has been shaken."

A muscle worked in Zach's jaw. "At her funeral, the pastor said that God gave us free will. And it was free will that allowed the likes of Fox to kill my sister."

"And despite my mother's devotion to her faith, she, too, was murdered." The familiar guilt weighed heavy on her chest. It wasn't fair to push her faith. Zach had to find his own way through his grief and feelings of guilt. Much as she had struggled. Much as she *still* struggled.

But wasn't that part of faith?

Heather dried the last glass and placed it in the cabinet. The Woodruffs and the Hopkinses were on a buggy tour of Quail Hollow, while Fiona had settled into a rocking chair in the sitting room with her laptop.

"I'll start making apple pie for dessert. I think I have everything set in the kitchen for now," Ruthie said, giving Heather a pointed stare.

Heather recognized a dismissal when she heard it, but still she pressed. "What can I do to help?"

"You hired me to take care of the kitchen and meals. Let me do that. I have to earn my keep."

Heather dried her hands on a dishrag. She didn't want to offend Ruthie by suggesting she couldn't manage her job.

"I'll go…" To do what, she wasn't exactly sure, until she found herself in the sitting room watching Fiona type away on her laptop. The young woman's back was to her. An unexpected whisper of dread made the hairs on the back of her neck prickle to life. She wasn't sure why. Perhaps because the memory of Fiona eagerly sharing the Quail Hollow gossip unnerved her.

What is she really writing about?

Fiona stopped typing and clasped her hands, but didn't turn around. "I can't type when someone's watching me."

Heather cringed. She hadn't meant to appear to be snooping. "Sorry, I didn't mean to interrupt." She turned to walk away, then stopped and decided to approach Fiona. "Why didn't you tell me you knew I was Brian Fox's ex-wife?"

Something flickered in Fiona's eyes, then she had the good sense to glance down. "You heard me talking." It wasn't framed as a question.

"I did."

"I'm sorry. I should have been more discreet."

Anger simmered just below the surface. "You shouldn't have been gossiping." Heather took another step closer. "What are you working on?" she asked, an edge to her tone.

"I've got my first contract to write a romance." Fiona smiled, a hint of an apology in her eyes. She turned the screen so Heather could read it. The passage read very much like something from a sweet romance novel. Heather's cheeks grew warm at the unfair accusation that had crossed her mind.

Fiona's eyes opened wide as she sensed it, too. "You thought maybe I was writing about you." She gave Heather an exaggerated frown, her eyes magnified behind her thick lenses. "I would never do something like that. I mean, I used to write articles for newspapers, but I'd never do something like that on the sly. That would be unethical."

Heather drew in a deep breath. "I value my privacy."

Fiona pushed her glasses up on her nose. "Yes, I understand completely. I just came here to work on my novel. That's all. It was inconsiderate of me to be all gossipy at breakfast this morning. I guess I enjoyed the attention too much when the other guests started asking questions."

Heather shrugged. "Well, I guess the cat is already out of the bag. The guests may have questions. I'll have to come up with some answers."

Fiona shifted the laptop and frowned. "I wasn't thinking. I'm sorry." She tapped her chin with her fingers. "I thought you should know I read about your mother's murder when I was doing research on Quail Hollow after I found this bed-and-breakfast."

"Oh." Pinpricks blanketed Heather's scalp.

"If you're ever interested, *that* would make a fantastic true crime story. I'd be honored to write it. I'm sure it would be a bestseller. A murder in Amish country..." A faraway look descended into Fiona's eyes as the wheels of her mind turned.

Heather rubbed her arm as unease skittered across her flesh. "I like my privacy." She didn't care that her words came out clipped. They had already been through this.

"Of course. I'm sorry. I don't mean to be insensitive."

"Thank you. I appreciate that and I'd appreciate your continued discretion." Heather lifted her hand to the laptop, suddenly feeling very disconcerted. "I'll let you get back to work. On your romance."

Fiona's eyebrows flew up. "Do you read them?"

Heather smiled, still having a hard time

figuring out this young woman. "Yes. I read across all genres. Haven't made much time for it lately, but now that the renovations are done, maybe I'll have more."

"You should also start one of those lending libraries for guests. The ones where they can take a book, leave a book. You could put shelves right in this room."

"That's a great idea." A few books would add charm to the mostly barren room. But Heather didn't want to overdecorate, which would be out of character for an Amish home.

Fiona leaned over and pulled a book from her bag resting against the rocker. "I'm almost finished with this one. I'll leave it here when I'm done. It can be your first lending library book."

"Sounds like a plan." Heather slid her fingers in the back pockets of her jeans. "Well, I better get a few things done before our guests return."

"If it's okay with you, I'll take my writing and my dinner up to my room later today." She lifted her laptop as if to prove a point. "I'm on deadline."

"Of course, I can bring something up."

"Oh no, I can come down and grab a plate. I just wanted you to know my plans so it wouldn't seem rude when I didn't join the other guests."

"This is your vacation. Do whatever makes you comfortable."

"Thank you." Fiona placed her fingers on the home row of the keyboard, but she didn't start typing. She turned to look at Heather. "I'm sorry if I caused you any pain by being gossipy. I'm not usually like that."

Heather tapped the door frame with her open palm. "Don't worry about it."

"Can I ask you something, though?" Fiona gave her a blank look.

"Okay." Heather didn't want to be rude, but she felt herself bracing for the question.

"Should I be worried that the escaped prisoner is going to come here? I mean, you hear stories all the time about innocent people getting caught up in domestic situations. Wrong place, wrong time sort of thing."

Heather had to focus on her breathing to control the anxiety that was welling up inside her. "We have reason to believe Brian Fox is dead."

Fiona's eyebrows shot up above the frame of her glasses and she had to catch her laptop before it slid off her lap.

"Really? What happened?" She clutched both sides of her laptop and a hint of apprehension flashed in her eyes.

"I can't really say, but law enforcement believes it's just a matter of time before they find his body."

"Oh." She lowered the lid of her laptop.

"How does that make you feel? I mean, you were married to him."

Heather stared at this woman. Under normal circumstances, she wouldn't entertain such personal questions from a stranger, but this was a paying guest. What did she owe her? "The true Brian Fox is an evil person. He tricked me. And unfortunately, his own free will led him to wherever he is today."

"Dead?"

She prayed he was dead.

"Yes, he's most likely dead."

"Hmm." Fiona seemed to consider this information. "Well, it seems you've found yourself a great guy in Zach. I was chatting with him earlier."

Heather suddenly felt flushed and she wanted nothing more than to end this discussion. Her guest certainly knew how to interrogate someone. Maybe she had missed her calling as a reporter.

"Yes, he's very helpful doing projects around the house." Zach and she had agreed they wouldn't let any of the guests know he was in law enforcement. They didn't want to make them feel uncomfortable or worried.

Fiona adjusted the monitor on her laptop, then looked up at Heather. "That's great. Well,

I shouldn't have pried. I talk too much sometimes."

Heather smiled tightly. "It's okay. But I'd rather not discuss the situation anymore, especially not in front of the other guests. Unless they have questions."

"Of course."

Heather turned to walk away. "Let either Ruthie or I know if you need anything."

"I will." Her fingers started flying across the keyboard before Heather reached the stairs.

Heather retreated upstairs and opened the medicine cabinet. It was empty save for the pain reliever. Zach had taken the ring for safekeeping.

A nervous energy she couldn't shake had her searching the entire room until she was satisfied that Brian hadn't left her any other unwanted gifts.

ELEVEN

A few days later, Zach toed his work boots off at the back door of the bed-and-breakfast and slipped inside. He drummed his fingers on his cell phone in his jacket pocket as he searched for Heather. He found her sitting at the rolltop desk making a few entries in the leather binder. The house had quieted down since the weekend guests had departed and he was grateful his boss had given him permission to stay in Quail Hollow for another week because it seemed like they were just about to get a break.

Heather ran her hand over the page and turned around; a smile lit her warm brown eyes. "The place is booking up. I might be able to make a go of this after all."

"I had no doubt you would." He leaned his shoulder against the door frame, hesitant to ruin the mood. But he had to tell her. He cleared his throat. "I received a phone call."

Heather slowly closed the book and turned to stare at him, taking in shallow breaths. "Tell me."

"A body's been found."

"A body? Brian's body?"

Zach held up his hand to caution her. "They believe it's him."

She threaded her fingers together and placed them in her lap, a show of restraint. Fox had done a number on her and now his delayed capture was tearing her up inside. Perhaps she didn't want to get her hopes up that this nightmare was officially over, however tragic the end result.

"I don't understand." She bit her lower lip. "Did something happen to the body? Why can't they identify it?"

Zach scrubbed a hand across his face, debating how many grisly details to share. But she deserved the truth. He crossed the room and sat down on the edge of a rocker. "Are you sure you want to hear the specifics?"

She stared at him with a steely expression. "I have to hear."

Zach nodded slightly, then said, "His face was destroyed. Deputy Gates mentioned that he had multiple wounds, including a gunshot to the face."

"If you hit him in the head, wouldn't they

have found his body in the water when they searched it?"

"A working theory is that he survived the initial wounds, but then killed himself to hasten the end when he got desperate. He'd been on the run for a long time."

All the color seemed to drain from her face. "That doesn't sound like Brian. I think he'd chew off his arm before ending his life. How do they figure it's him?"

"Same general description—height, weight—and he had on his orange prison uniform under a jacket."

Heather slowly stood and put her hand down on the corner of the desk to steady herself. "Can I see the body?"

"I don't think that's a good idea. That's an image you'll never be able to get out of your head." Zach stood, watching her carefully.

"There are a lot of images I can't get out of my head. As warped as it sounds, knowing he can't hurt me again will give me great comfort." The tremble in her voice and the slight sway of her body weren't very convincing, but who was he to deny her this request?

"Where's Ruthie?" he asked, stalling. "Don't you two have work to do around here?"

"She's working in the greenhouse today."

Heather crossed her arms and continued to press. "I need to see the body."

He stared at her a long moment before pulling his phone out of his pocket. "I'll call Deputy Gates."

"No, let's just show up. Harder to say no."

"I don't think this is a good idea," he repeated.

"Please."

"Okay. Grab your jacket."

Breathe in. Breathe out. Breathe in. Breathe out.

Heather tugged on her seat belt as Zach talked on the cell phone, getting directions from a dispatcher as to the location of the body. From what she could hear, personnel were still on location, bringing Brian's body out of the woods. Maybe Zach was right—maybe this was a bad idea.

But a stubbornness deep inside wouldn't let her admit her mistake. No, not a mistake. She was just afraid. She had to see for herself that Brian was dead, thus allowing her to live a life without fear. She couldn't bear to continue always wondering *what if.*

"You okay?" Zach asked when he ended the call and dropped the phone in the empty cup holder.

"I've been better."

"You don't have to do this."

"I know." She turned to face the window as trees, cornfields and the occasional house zipped by. She sat up straighter when she recognized where they were headed. "This is the direction of the Hershbergers' home. They didn't find him, did they?"

"No, the body was found by an elderly man walking his dog in the hills behind their house."

A new flush of dread washed over her. Had Brian been watching her when she had taken sanctuary there? She swallowed back her fear, praying she'd make it through the next moment. Then the next. One moment at a time.

They drove past the Hershbergers' home. There was no sign of anyone outside. About a half mile away, a dozen law enforcement vehicles, ranging from the local sheriff's department to New York State troopers, lined the shoulder of the road. Zach pulled in behind an ambulance. There'd be no need for that.

Heather reached for the door handle and Zach touched her knee. "Wait in the car?"

"I didn't come all this way to wait in the car." Besides, with her nerves, she was ready to jump out of her skin. She needed to get out and expend some of her nervous energy.

Zach met her around her side of the car and

they approached the edge of the woods. A trooper stopped them from going any farther. "You'll have to wait here."

Heather let out a long breath, her stomach churning. A buzzing started deep in her head, much as it had when she was married to Brian and she feared him going off on her for no other reason than she used wheat bread instead of white. Or some equally frivolous reason that always kept her in a state of watchful anticipation.

"You don't look so good. We can wait in the car." Zach's voice sounded strange, as if he were standing far away and talking softly through a long tunnel.

"No. Just help me get through this...I have to do this."

Zach touched the small of her back and she fought every instinct to bury her face in his shoulder and let him protect her. Let him take all her fear and worry away. But she refused to be weak. A long time ago she had vowed to not rely on anyone but herself.

As she stood next to Zach, she stared up into the trees, a beautiful palette of oranges, reds and yellows, wondering how long Brian had been this close. *Was* he watching her when she was staying with Ruthie? The idea struck terror in her heart.

Breathe in. Breathe out.

Voices coming from the woods grew louder. Then flashes of orange caught her eye. Her adrenaline spiked. *Can I do this?*

Deputy Gates led the search team out of the woods. He was wearing an orange safety vest. He seemed to catch Zach's eye and made a direct line for them. "You shouldn't be here."

"I need to see the body," Heather rasped. The back of her throat ached.

The deputy slowly shook his head, looking to Zach for support. "Between the gunshot wound and animals, there's not a lot left. It's not a good idea."

Heather pressed the flat of her hand against her rioting belly and swallowed back her nausea.

"Can you give us more information about the hiker who found him?" Zach asked, shooting Heather a reassuring smile.

"An old-timer, George Campbell. Walks his dog everywhere. The dog stumbled across the remains. George called us in right away from his cell phone."

"Are you convinced it's him?" Zach asked.

The deputy ticked the items off on his fingers. "Peters Correctional Facility inmate uniform. Same height and build. And they're running the serial number on the gun they found with him." The officer's phone buzzed on his duty belt. "Hold up." He turned his back to them and took the call. His words swirled into a garbled mess, making her think of the old *Peanuts* cartoons when adults were speaking. She stared at the tree line, holding her breath, expecting men with a body bag to burst into the opening, wondering how she'd feel when they did. Relieved? Afraid? Sad?

The deputy turned back to them. "The serial number on the gun matches one of the guns stolen from a home near the correctional facility. The young woman who helped him escape is out on bail, but with strict instructions not to leave town."

Heather closed her eyes and nodded. "It seems everything's lining up."

"Yes. They'll run his dental records, which may take a few days, but I'm confident we have found Brian Fox."

"What do you think?" Heather asked Zach.

"I agree with the deputy. We've got him."

"I need to do this for my own peace of mind." Would refusing to see the body make her weak?

"Ma'am," the deputy said, "you wouldn't be able to identify anyone considering the condition of the body."

She felt Zach's gaze on her. Some of her conviction was draining out of her. "This is something I need to do." But really, she wasn't sure anymore.

"We'll run his dental records, which will make everything rock solid. Only a few more days and there'll be no doubt."

"What do you think?" Zach asked. "Please spare yourself the pain."

She looked up and met Zach's gaze, then slowly shifted her gaze to the men emerging from the woods. Rescuers carried a sled with a body bag. Her heart rate slowed in her chest as the world around her grew black. Only one image remained. The body bag.

Does it contain what's left of Brian?

The men stopped at the back of a black van. A man reached for the handle and opened the doors. They slid the body bag inside.

The body.

Heather's world swayed. She gently touched Zach's arm. "Let's go."

She didn't need to see the body. Brian was dead.

On the way home, Heather insisted they stop by the Hershbergers' farm to tell Ruthie and Maryann that her ex-husband no longer posed a threat to the quiet town of Quail Hollow.

They knocked on the front door, but no one answered.

"Let's try the greenhouse," Heather said.

They found them watering the mums. Emma was stacking empty pots in the back. Maryann saw them first. She turned off the hose and let her hands hang limply by her sides. Apparently their presence portended something really bad. "What is it?"

"Brian Fox is dead."

Ruthie's shoulders relaxed. "They finally found him. What a relief."

"Yes, that's why we wanted to let you know. They found him in the hills behind your home." Heather watched them closely.

"Oh, dear." Maryann glanced over toward her younger daughter, then back at them as she fidgeted with the folds of her long dress.

"No need to worry now," Zach said solemnly.

"Had you seen anyone out there lately?" Heather asked, still trying to wrap her brain around everything that had happened.

Maryann's eyes grew wide. "We were missing some eggs, but I assumed a critter had gotten into the henhouse. Do you think…?"

"There's really no way to know. But you're safe now." Zach touched the small of Heather's back, a gesture Heather found greatly reassuring.

Maryann stepped forward. "How are you? This hasn't been easy for you."

"No, it hasn't." She flattened her lips into a thin line, trying to tamp down her emotions. She had come here to reassure her dear friends, not to seek comfort from them. "I appreciate all your support through this. I don't know what I'd do without you. You've become like family."

Maryann smiled, her porcelain skin only a shade darker than her white bonnet. "Your mother would be so proud of how you handled yourself through all this." She clasped her hands. "You *are* part of this family."

A lump of emotion clogged Heather's throat. What she wouldn't do to have known her mother. Getting to know her mother's best friend was what she'd have to settle for. But she considered getting to know Maryann and her daughters to be a true blessing.

Ruthie smiled. "I love working for you, too. I have to tell you, though, I've been a nervous wreck since I first learned that man had escaped from prison. So glad he's not going to be a problem anymore."

"Now you can run the bed-and-breakfast without worrying," Maryann said. "You'll experience the Quail Hollow that we all know. It's usually so quiet and peaceful."

"I look forward to it," Heather said, suddenly feeling warm under the intensity of the sun through the glass of the greenhouse.

"Your mother always seemed so restless here, but I just know you won't feel that way. Not now."

An unease whispered across Heather's brain. *Restless?* Heather's father had assured her that her mother had been nothing but loving and doted on her children. Perhaps Maryann had misspoken. But now wasn't the time to get into that. Brian was finally gone.

Gone. Dead.

Guilt twisted in her heart. She shouldn't be happy that he was dead. What kind of person did that make her?

"Does that mean you're going home, Marshal Walker?" Ruthie's question snapped Heather out of her maudlin thoughts.

Heather shot her friend daggers but found herself holding her breath waiting for his answer. But what did she expect? Of course he'd be going home. Brian was no longer a threat. She was no longer in danger.

She glanced down at her fingernails, pretending not to care about his answer.

"Yes, my boss had given me a week extension to stay in town, but now that the case is resolved, he'll be looking for me to get back to the office."

"When will you be leaving?" Heather wished

she could take the question back. She hadn't meant to sound so needy.

He met her eyes and their gazes lingered. "I should probably head back in the morning."

The single word "oh" flew out of her mouth.

"Sounds like someone would like you to hang around."

"Ruthie!" both Maryann and Heather said in unison in similar scolding tones.

"What?" Ruthie's eyes grew wide, but she didn't look sorry in the least. Lowering her head to hide her grin, she deadheaded the nearest mum.

"Will we see you again, Zach?" Maryann asked in a motherly tone. "It was so nice to meet you."

"I own a cabin in the woods nearby. I'll make sure to stop by and say hello when I'm in town."

"That would be nice," Maryann said.

"I'm actually going there tonight," Zach said. "Make sure it's closed up before I head back home."

Heather drew back her shoulders and pointed at Ruthie. "Why don't you stay here tonight with your family? I'll pick you up tomorrow afternoon."

"Sounds good." Ruthie brushed the dirt off her hands. "Thank you."

Heather and Zach said their goodbyes, then

walked out to climb into his truck. She buckled in and sighed, perhaps a little too loudly.

"I could wait until Sunday night to go back to Buffalo if you need help. My boss wasn't expecting me till Monday. The roof on the barn is only partially finished, but Sloppy Sam said he'd get it done."

Heather shook her head, perhaps a little too adamantly. "Yes, the Amish work crew will do a great job. I can't keep you from your work."

"Can I take you for something to eat?" Zach asked as he pulled out onto the main road.

"Do you think we could pick up a pizza in town? I'm drained. I'd rather relax at home instead of sitting in a restaurant."

"Sounds good. If you don't mind, why don't you call ahead? We'll pick it up on the way home. We'll eat, then I'll go to my cabin for the night."

As Heather searched for her phone at the bottom of her purse, she had myriad emotions crowding her soul. She'd miss Zach. But it was time she faced her future as a confident young woman.

Without relying on a man.

Zach slid the pizza box on top of the stove. The smell of cheese and pepperoni reached his nose and made his stomach growl. He was hungrier than he had realized.

"Would you like some pop?" Heather asked as she stretched up into the cabinet and pulled out some paper plates. It was the most she had spoken since they had picked up the pizza. He had written it off as exhaustion from all the stress. "I have a few kinds here. Is a cola okay?"

"Sounds good."

She poured two glasses of cola and he plated two pieces of pizza. They settled in at the table next to one another enjoying the view through the new window overlooking the barn and the rest of the yard awash in the early-evening glow of the setting sun. With her food sitting untouched in front of her, she smiled. "This is just the view I imagined and this is the first time I've taken the time to enjoy it. Really enjoy it without the nagging dread that Brian was out there." She tilted her head and a light came into her eyes. "This is the first time that I've been allowed to enjoy it."

Zach's gaze drifted to the corner where they had found the graffiti the escaped convict had left. Zach had a hard time thinking of Fox as this beautiful woman's ex-husband. As his smart little sister's husband. The man had duped a lot of people, including the woman at the correctional facility who helped him escape. She was currently out on bail. But she wasn't his concern. The legal system would take care of her.

Making sure Fox couldn't hurt any more people had been his goal. After dinner, he planned to call Deputy Gates and find out where they had taken Fox's body. Even though he had talked Heather out of viewing his remains. *He* had to see them. *He* had to be convinced.

Zach took a bite of his pizza and the two of them sat in companionable silence as they ate.

"I've come a long way since the night you showed up at my back door." Heather's tone had a distant quality to it.

"You've always been a strong woman. From the first time I met you."

"If I had been braver, your sister would still be alive."

Zach put his piece of pizza down, realizing neither of them was going to eat until they had this discussion.

"You can't blame yourself. If you had stayed, you may have died. And you had no way of warning my sister. You didn't know. You have to move forward."

She traced the rim of her glass. "I'll never forget your father's face at the trial. He was destroyed."

A pang of guilt knotted his stomach. No one

had empathized more with his father's pain than he had. As the big brother—in law enforcement, no less—he should have protected his sister.

"There's enough bad feelings to go around." He reached over and took her hand. "Let's move forward. It's over."

She turned to him and met his eyes. "It really is, isn't it?"

"Yeah. It is." He leaned closer and paused. A small smile played on her lips and she leaned closer to him. He brushed a gentle kiss across his lips. She tasted sweet from the cola.

He pulled back and looked into her eyes. A flicker of happiness danced in their depths, having replaced the fear and worry. She lifted her hand and cupped his cheek. "Thank you for being here."

Her fingers slid from his cheek and picked up her slice of pizza. "I guess we should finish up here. You probably have to pack for home."

He nodded and took another bite of his pizza, but he had suddenly lost his appetite.

Apparently his job here was done.

It was time to go home.

TWELVE

Heather woke up early to the sound of rumbling thunder in the distance. She rolled over and snuggled into her covers, trying to put her finger on the emotion she was feeling. Hope? Renewal? Empty? Last night with Zach hadn't exactly gone as planned. She hadn't anticipated his kiss as they sat at the table enjoying pizza.

She threw back the covers and climbed out of bed. The kiss had sent tingles all the way to her toes, but she wasn't the type to have a fleeting romance. And based on her past experience, she probably wasn't the type to have any romance. She didn't trust her judgment when it came to men. She had been so, *so* wrong before.

But Zach was nothing like Brian.

Heather slipped into the bathroom and chuckled at her reflection in the mirror. Based on the every-which-way of her hair, she must have tossed and turned all night. With more than a little effort, she ran a comb through her long tresses. She had a quiet morning planned before all her guests arrived tomorrow afternoon. Five women were registered for a weekend getaway, but the weather didn't look like it was going to cooperate. Maybe with Ruthie's help she'd try a new soup for Saturday afternoon.

Twisting her hair up in a ponytail, she left her bedroom—leaving the door unlocked—and headed downstairs. The clock on the kitchen wall ticked away each second. The red light on the alarm pad indicated it was set. That was when she saw a piece of paper on the table. From Zach. Funny, she hadn't noticed it last night after he left.

She picked up the scrap of paper and realized it was his business card. She ran her thumb over the embossed letters of his name. Their relationship had been a professional one despite a little kiss.

That's all.

She frowned. Her heart disagreed. She should have felt more content. Safe, at least, after knowing her ex-husband was no longer out there. But instead she felt...lonely.

You won't feel lonely come tomorrow afternoon when the bed-and-breakfast is buzzing with guests. Enjoy this moment.

She grabbed a bowl of cereal and sat at the

table overlooking the yard. The exact spot where she had sat with Zach twelve hours ago. The exact spot where he had kissed her. She touched her lips, remembering the warmth of his mouth on hers.

Why was she so quick to dismiss the notion of a relationship with him? He was a good man.

She was damaged goods.

Instead of obsessing, she focused on finishing her breakfast. She couldn't just wander around the house all morning, missing Zach, listening to the rain beat on the roof. She had to do something. She wasn't scheduled to pick up Ruthie until this afternoon.

Her gaze drifted to the barn. That was when she knew what she had to do. Soon, the news coverage of Brian Fox would be a distant memory. Perhaps now was the time to focus on putting another tragedy behind her.

She put her bowl in the sink, then grabbed her rain jacket off the hook, stuffed her feet in her Wellies and headed outside. The cool autumn rain felt refreshing on her cheeks. She turned and locked the door behind her. Some things would die a slow death. However, she supposed locking doors and setting alarms were a smart way of life for any woman living alone.

She crossed the yard. Determination lead her

toward the open barn door. She swallowed back her nausea. The dilapidated barn taunted her, as if it had taken on a life of its own.

"You can do this," she muttered to herself. The familiar tingling of a threatening panic attack bit at her fingertips. She glanced up. "*Mem*, stay with me. Help me do this so I can move forward."

Letting out a long breath through narrowed lips, she kept up her steady pace for fear she'd chicken out. The muddy path sucked the soles of her rain boots with every step. When she reached the open door, a chill slithered down her spine. With trembling fingers, it took her a few tries to catch the zipper on her raincoat and yank it up to her neck. Pulling her sleeves down over her hands, she slipped inside the barn. Her mouth went dry. She walked over to the horses' stalls. There were three of them.

Heather had no idea in which one her mother's body had been found. Tears stung her eyes as she peered into each one. She ran her hand along the half door, vowing to put the barn repairs at the top of her priority list. Her mother had loved horses.

Zach had already made a good start.

A horse or two would be a wonderful addition. She'd have to repair the fences, too, so they could safely roam the property. That was about the extent of what she knew about horses, but she figured Ruthie would be a wealth of information.

Heather swiped away at the tears and said a silent prayer for her mother. That she would rest in peace. And that Heather'd be able to live with not knowing what happened because sometimes there were no answers. She had to ask God for comfort and peace.

The sound of shuffling made Heather spin around. Icy dread coursed through her veins. She squinted into the heavy shadows as thunder rumbled overhead and a bolt of lightning made her jump.

Crossing her arms, she decided the noises she had heard were the settlings of a very old building during a storm. She turned to leave the barn when someone yanked a burlap bag over her head and threw her down onto the ground. Her elbow and hip slammed into the hard-packed dirt.

Her scream got lodged in her throat as she sucked in the gritty fabric of the burlap. Panic consumed all rational thought.

Before she had a chance to gain her bearings, someone jumped on top of her and tied her hands behind her back. As the person yanked Heather to her feet, Heather pleaded, "Stop. Why are you doing this?" Shadows moved quickly, masked by the heavy weave of the burlap.

The image of her mother, the one she had held in her six-year-old brain, floated to mind. Was she going to meet her Maker in the same place as her mother's body had been found?

Fear made it nearly impossible to think. Her pulse whooshed in her ears, masking the subtle sounds swirling around her.

Heather was shoved a few feet and tossed to the ground again. She whimpered in pain but refused to give up. In a desperate attempt to escape, Heather bucked and kicked, but her attacker had the upper hand. Something hard came down across her head, the blinding pain making her nauseous and dizzy.

"Stop." The single word was slurred, sounding as if it hadn't come from her mouth. "Please."

The attacker used his advantage to tie her feet together. She struggled to see, but between the burlap and the heavy shadows and the throbbing pain in her skull, she couldn't make out more than shadows.

"Brian? Please." The words sounded hoarse as they rasped out of her throat.

Brian's dead. Isn't he?

A strange sound floated in the air. *Is that me sobbing?*

Her attacker dragged her as she bucked with her bound legs, unable to free herself. "Stop! Please!"

The attacker dropped her legs. Heather's attempt to scoot back was made more difficult by her bound hands and feet. Something slammed her in the head again.

She fell back. Her head slammed against the ground. Nausea welled up and her head throbbed as she struggled to maintain consciousness.

Please, dear Lord. Save me. Save me.

The sound of liquid splashing on the ground filled her ears and the smell of gasoline gagged her.

Oh no... Oh no...

Panic, and a concussion, no doubt, made her dizzy.

Her ears buzzed, but she heard the unmistakable sound of a match hissing to life.

Zach paced the small lobby of the sheriff's office waiting for Deputy Gates to return. Zach glanced at his watch. It was early, but the deputy had assured him he'd meet him here, even at this hour.

Impatience made him antsy. He knocked on the glass separating the common man from those who protected and served, an added security measure necessary in modern times. Quail Hollow wasn't immune to evil.

"Deputy Gates is on his way," the young woman said as she hung up the phone.

"Okay." Zach squared his shoulders, bracing himself for what he had asked Deputy Gates to meet him for. He had to see Fox's body. He couldn't leave any room for doubt.

Crossing his arms, he turned toward the window. A sheriff's patrol car pulled up and Deputy Gates climbed out. Zach yanked the door open and met his new friend outside.

"Morning," Zach said, biting back his frustration when he noticed the deputy reaching into the cruiser to pull out a tray of coffees.

"Morning," the deputy said. "Coffee?" He held out the tray.

Zach waved him off. "No." He opened the door to the office for the deputy, who seemed determined to keep walking, perhaps to get out of the rain. "Deputy, I was hoping to see Fox's body."

A buzzing sounded and the deputy opened the interior door to the secure offices. "Come on in."

Zach didn't want to go into the sheriff's headquarters. He wanted the deputy to escort him to the morgue. He could have gone himself, but he thought using local law enforcement would go over better. Besides, he had no official reason to see Brian's body. This was personal. Deputy Gates was his in. Less questions this way.

"Come back to my office." The deputy led him through a series of hallways to a cubicle in the center of a large office space, dropping off two coffees on his way. He slid the tray with one remaining coffee on his desk. "Sure you don't want one?"

Zach smiled tightly and finally accepted the coffee. "Thanks." He took a long sip, hoping the caffeine would fix his mood. "Now, about our phone call."

The deputy sat and rested his elbows on his knees. "That's why I brought you back here. News is going to hit soon enough, but we need to try to get a jump on him."

A ticking started in Zach's jaw. "What are you talking about?" The coffee suddenly felt sour in his gut.

"Fox's dentist expedited his X-rays."

"Yeah?"

"The body. It's not Fox's. The dental records don't match."

Zach slowly leaned back, the reality of the latest discovery washing over him.

"Who is it?"

"Too early to tell, but a young man went

missing about twenty miles outside of Peters Correctional Facility. Law enforcement didn't connect the two until now. They're sending us the young man's dental records to see if it's him."

"Brian found someone roughly his height and build and faked his own suicide."

The deputy ran his hands up and down his thighs. "He's smart enough to know we'd figure it out. Far as I can tell. He was trying to buy time."

Buy time.

The last two words bounced around Zach's head. *Buy time.* He slammed down his coffee, the contents of the cup sloshing over the edges.

"What's going on?"

"Send patrols to the Quail Hollow Bed & Breakfast on Lapp Road. I have to go. I have to get to Heather."

The tires on Zach's truck spit out gravel as he tore out of the sheriff's parking lot. He had to get to Heather. *Now!* He grabbed his cell phone and dialed Heather's phone number. Not a great idea while racing down a country road, but it couldn't be avoided.

He put the phone on speaker and the hollow echo of the ringing phone bounced around the interior of his vehicle.

"Come on, Heather. Answer, answer, *an-*

swer..." He tapped the side of his steering wheel as anxiety charged through him.

Heather's voice sounded in his car speakers. "Hi, you've reached Quail Hollow Bed & Breakfast. Please leave your name and number and we'll get back to you. We look forward to your visit."

"Heather," Zach yelled, as if she might hear him despite the fact he was talking into her voice mail. "Call me as soon as you get this. The body was not Fox's. The dental records do not match. Lock the doors. Make sure the alarm is set. I'll be there in—" he glanced at the clock out of habit "—five minutes."

Zach ended the call and pressed the accelerator to the floor and the engine hummed. In the not-so-far distance behind him, he could hear sirens. He hoped they were racing to Lapp Road and not to pull him over for driving like a lunatic.

With a white-knuckled grip, he navigated the curve on Lapp Road. Up ahead, smoke filled the air in a thick black plume disappearing into the dark storm clouds. His heart plummeted.

"God, I know I haven't prayed since before Jill died, but if You have any mercy on a poor soul like me, please, spare Heather. *Please.*"

His truck skidded on the wet pavement as he slowed at Heather's driveway. His truck bobbled over the ruts. He slammed the gear into Park and jumped out of the truck, leaving the door open and the engine running. He leaned into the bed of the truck and snapped a fire extinguisher off the brace holding it in place, grateful he had gotten his truck back from the collision shop.

He ran as fast as he could, feeling like he was approaching a forest fire with a squirt gun. But he needed something. God was guiding his actions. He just knew Heather was in the barn.

He yanked the pin out of the extinguisher and aimed it at the door and white foam coated the frame, but flames licked the dry wood farther in.

"Heather! Heather!" Zach screamed, then he hooked his arm over his nose and mouth and pushed into the smoky confines of the barn. Holding his breath, he went in farther until he kicked something soft.

Dropping to all fours, he breathed in a shallow breath and coughed, his lungs filling with the acrid smoke. He reached out and felt an arm. He felt around her shoulders, slid his hands under her armpits and dragged her out of the barn.

A wave of relief washed over him when he saw Heather's chest rise and fall once he set her on the grass a good thirty feet from the barn. He tugged off the burlap bag from over her head and his heart dropped when he saw the blood around her hairline.

Out of the corner of his eye, he saw the deputy running across the lawn. Zach hollered to him, "Call an ambulance!"

"On the way." The deputy approached, hands fisted on his hips as he scanned the landscape. "Is Miss Miller okay?"

"Heather, it's Zach. You're going to be okay." He worked on the ropes that bound her hands and feet. When she started to cough, he helped her sit up.

"Water," Heather rasped.

Zach was vaguely aware of the deputy instructing someone to get her water. As he helped support her into a seated position, he scanned the landscape. Fox could be anywhere.

Zach pointed frantically at Deputy Gates. "Have your men search the fields. He can't be far."

"Who?" Heather coughed again.

"Fox."

Her eyes widened in her sooty face as rain plastered her hair to her scalp. She slowly closed her eyes and her body went limp. Carefully, Zach laid her down. A fear like he'd never known spiked through him. He couldn't lose Heather.

"Is that ambulance on the way?" he yelled.

The deputy spoke into his shoulder radio and then listened. "Two minutes out."

Zach slid his arms under Heather's armpits and knees and hoisted her up. Her head lolled against his chest. "Come on, honey. I've got you." He ran toward the driveway and heard the sound of approaching sirens, his footing unstable over the muddy terrain. "I've got you," he repeated over and over.

He reached the ambulance just as it stopped in front of the house. The paramedic jumped out and swung open the back doors. "What do you have here?"

"Smoke inhalation. Possible head injury."

Zach climbed into the back of the ambulance and laid an unconscious Heather on the stretcher. "I'm going with her. Can I close these doors? We have to get moving."

"Yeah, yeah," the paramedic said as she started working on her.

As Zach reached to close the back door, he realized with a sick feeling in the pit of his stomach that his truck was missing. It was possible someone had moved it, but he knew better. The search party wasn't going to find Fox in the fields because Fox had gotten away in Zach's truck.

Zach sat down on the bench next to Heather

in the back of the ambulance. He pulled out his cell phone to notify the deputy of the new development. It helped to focus on details. Job-related tasks. Made him feel like he was accomplishing something when deep down he knew he was helpless when it came to what mattered most: Heather.

Zach ended the call and leaned forward, resting his elbows on his knees. He reached out and took Heather's limp hand in his and pressed her cold fingers to his lips.

Dear Lord, let her be okay.

THIRTEEN

The stink of the acrid smoke lingered in Heather's nose while a steady *thump-thump-thump* throbbed behind her eyes as she dreamed a million bizarre dreams of disjointed nonsense: swinging on a tire swing while pumping her legs toward the sky with a long dress flapping around her legs; serving guests at a long table that extended toward the horizon like one of those infinity pools; someone reaching for her through black smoke with strong arms.

Distant voices lulled her out of her strange dreams. It seemed to take a herculean effort to open her eyes. The voices grew louder and then grew distant again.

Finally prying her eyes open, she immediately regretted it as the long fluorescent lights in the ceiling were like a million pinpricks to her eyeballs.

"Ohh…"

A shadow crossed her face and a warm, gentle hand touched the back of hers. "I'm right here." It was Zach.

She tried again to open her eyes. This time, Zach's handsome face blocked the harsh lighting. He reached toward her and slid a piece of hair off her forehead. "Hey there. You had us worried."

"What…?" The memories of her attack assaulted her brain like a tsunami unexpectedly taking her legs out from under her.

"How long have I been here?" The intensity in Zach's gaze unnerved her.

"Twelve hours." He lowered himself into the chair next to her bed and a strange thought ran through her mind. Had Zach been by her side the whole time?

"Who attacked me?" She tried to lift her arm and she realized there were wires coming out of her hand. "What aren't you telling me?"

Zach took her hand in both of his. "Brian Fox is alive."

She tried to push up on her elbow and immediately regretted it when nausea rolled over her. "What?" She furrowed her brow. "Can you elevate the top of my bed? I need to sit up." This wasn't the kind of news a person took lying down.

Zach found the control and pressed the button and the top of the bed moved up as the motor hummed. Heather folded her hands on top of her stomach as she talked herself out of a panic attack. "What about the body pulled out of the woods?" Tears threatened, but she refused to give her ex-husband any more of her tears.

"Fox wanted us to think the body was his. Made it look like he committed suicide by shooting off his face. Then he had the added benefit of time. Bodies decompose. Animals…" Zach seemed to be measuring his words, but Heather didn't want to be coddled. She needed the truth.

"How did they figure it out?"

"When they finally got his dental records early this morning, law enforcement realized their mistake. I was on my way to tell you when I spotted the fire."

"You pulled me out of the fire?"

He nodded.

"Thank you." She blinked slowly. Thank God for putting him in her path.

"You didn't see him when he attacked you?"

"No." She ran a hand across her forehead. "Someone came up behind me and put a burlap bag over my head. He whacked me with something." She pressed her fingers delicately to her sore cheekbone. A small smile flickered at the corners of her mouth. "I can only imagine what I look like."

Zach tilted his head and stared intently at her, cupping her cheek gingerly with his hand. "I've never seen a more beautiful sight. I thought I lost you."

"You thought you lost me?" She hadn't meant to say the words out loud.

He ran his hand over his mouth. "I'm grateful I learned the truth and raced back to the bed-and-breakfast in time."

"Yeah, me, too." She leaned back on the pillow and groaned as the room spun around her. "The bed-and-breakfast. I have guests arriving tomorrow. Tomorrow, right?" She strained to orient herself. *What day is it?*

"Ruthie contacted them to cancel."

"I can—" The pain that shot through her head stole her breath away.

He gently placed his hand on her shoulder and helped her settle back in. "Even if you were physically able to run the bed-and-breakfast right now, the smell from the barn fire is heavy inside the house."

"Oh no." Heather blinked furiously, determined to keep the tears at bay.

Zach slid his hand down her arm and stopped at her hand. "Shh," he said, swiping his thumb back and forth across the palm of her hand.

"Other than the barn, there's no damage to the house. Nothing that a little fresh air won't fix."

"Are you sure?"

"Yeah. Focus on getting better."

Heather raised her eyebrows. "Easy for you to say." She licked her top lip. It felt dry. Anticipating her needs, Zach reached over and poured some water from the pitcher into a plastic cup. The ice rattled as he held the straw to her lips. "Thanks."

Just then voices grew louder outside her door. Passing doctors or nurses. That was what she must have heard during her fitful sleep.

"Did the doctor say how long I had to stay here?"

"Okay, about that…"

"What?"

"I told a little white lie and said you were my fiancée. It was the only way I could get any answers. Even at that, I think she was afraid of breaking some sort of privacy laws, but she had mercy on me, I suppose."

"Okay, fine. How long?"

"Overnight."

"Oh." The thought of trying to get some sleep here with all the lights and sounds and… She supposed with a head injury, the doctor had to be careful. She tried to sound cheery. "I can go home tomorrow?"

"Not home. I assured the physician I'd take care of you."

She stared at him but didn't say anything.

"I'll take you to my cabin in the woods for a few days of rest and relaxation."

Heather sat in the passenger seat of Zach's borrowed truck with her eyes closed against the bright sunshine. Zach noticed she was finally able to open them when he turned up the long lane to his cabin. The mature trees created a canopy of darkness that seemed to provide some relief to her eyes.

"You doing okay? We're almost there."

"The doctor said the pain should gradually decrease each day. I'm looking forward to it." She let out an awkward laugh, obviously still in pain.

"Do you need me to get you anything? I can run out to the store."

"A comfortable place to rest and darkness."

"I can do that."

Zach parked the truck and ran around to her side to help her out. "I'll come back out for your bag." Ruthie had packed one for her.

Heather felt frail as he slid his arm around her back. He'd spent most of the previous night following up on leads on Fox. *Nothing.* His stolen truck hadn't even been spotted. Once he got

Heather safely settled at the cabin, he'd return to the search. He couldn't sit this one out.

He reached around her and twisted the doorknob to the cabin. The door swung open with a screech and his father scrambled out of a chair, the newspaper on his lap fluttering to the floor. Zach suspected his father had been dozing.

Heather paused in the doorway and glanced up at Zach, curiosity glistening in her eyes.

"Heather Miller, this is my father, Charlie Walker."

Heather offered her hand. "Hello."

"Nice to see you, Miss Miller. We met briefly during the trial."

Heather's face grew somber. "Of course, Mr. Walker. I remember." Her hands fluttered around the hollow of her neck as her gaze dropped to the floor.

"So," his father said, perhaps a little too cheerfully, "I hear you took a knock to the head."

Heather groaned. "I suppose I'm lucky I have a hard head."

"Come on in." Zach encouraged her forward with a hand to the small of her back. "Do you want to sit for a bit or would you rather lie down?"

His father bent and picked up the newspaper that had slid to the floor. "Sit here. It's the most comfortable chair. I'll get you some water." Without waiting for an answer, his father crossed the room to the kitchen.

Zach helped Heather settle into the oversize chair. He slid a blanket his mother had crocheted off the back of the chair and spread it across her lap. She looked frail and the bruise under her eye had turned a purplish yellow.

His father reappeared with a glass of ice water and set it on the table next to her. "Here you go."

His father stood off to the side. "Are you hungry? I make a pretty mean grilled cheese."

Heather smiled. The first time Zach had seen her genuinely smile since finding her in the smoke-filled barn. "I'm not hungry now, but can I take a rain check?"

"Absolutely." He drew in a deep breath and let it out. "I'm going to take a quick walk around the exterior of the house. Give you some time to settle in."

"Thanks, Dad."

His dad put on his boots and coat and disappeared outside.

Zach sat down on the footstool in front of Heather and leaned forward, resting his forearms on his thighs and clasping his hands together.

Heather slumped back in the chair and

groaned. "You're going out to look for Brian yourself, aren't you?"

"I have to. I can't—"

"Sit around babysitting me?" She must have recognized the bite to her tone and quickly added, "I'm sorry. That's not fair of me. It's just…" She adjusted the blanket on her lap. "I'm afraid."

Something told him she had rarely, if ever, admitted her fear. "My father is a retired marshal. He'll protect you."

Her gaze drifted to the door. "He's doing more than stretching his legs outside."

"Yeah, he's checking the property for any signs of Fox."

She drew in a deep breath and closed her eyes. "You have to find him. I can't live like this anymore."

Heather clamped her jaw trying to stop it from trembling. She wanted to be strong for Zach, but she was tired. Tired of hiding. Tired of hurting. Tired of wondering what was going to happen next.

So, so tired.

"I need to join the search party," Zach said.

"I get it." Heather tried to reassure him with a smile, but all she wanted to do was cry and take comfort in Zach's arms. But how was that fair when she was here and his sister was dead? At the hands of the man he needed to find.

Zach patted her knee. "Call me if you need anything." He frowned. "Cell reception out here is hit-and-miss. But there's a landline."

"And I'm here." Mr. Walker had come back in from outside, his nose red from the cold. He pulled back one side of his coat, revealing a gun. "I won't let anything happen to you on my watch."

Zach crossed the room to where his father stood. He clapped his father on the shoulder. "I don't anticipate any trouble, since this place isn't listed anywhere. Fox would have no way of tracking you here."

"But you found me." She hated the subtle tremble in her voice.

"We tracked you down through a real estate transaction. The land for this cabin was purchased by my grandmother. It would be impossible for Fox to make that connection." Zach snatched his coat from the arm of the couch. "I'll bring your bag in, then hit the road."

"Okay." Her mind raced, but she couldn't think of anything else to say. It wasn't fair of her to keep him any longer.

Mr. Walker sat on the couch and leaned over and opened a drawer on the coffee table. It was filled with old VHS tapes. "Feel like a movie?"

She didn't. But she didn't want to be rude.

"I might close my eyes, but I wouldn't mind the background noise." It might help distract her.

A minute later, Zach breezed back in. "I'll put your bag in the guest bedroom." He stopped on his way back through the cabin. "Last call. Need anything?"

She shook her head and immediately regretted it as pain ricocheted through her head.

"I'll check in. Keep you posted," he said, as much to her as to his father.

Heather heard the lock snap into place. Mr. Walker put a movie in and Heather found herself drifting off to sleep.

She wasn't sure how long she had been dozing when the smell of something on the stove pulled her out of her disjointed dreams. She opened her eyes and sat up and groaned at the pain. She tried to rub the crick out of her neck, but the pain persisted. She feared the only way she could get rid of this pain entirely was to obtain a time machine and go back to before Brian took a board to her head.

But why did he cover her head? Brian was the kind of guy who liked to see the fear in her eyes when he hurt her. She pulled herself upright and rested her elbow on the arm of the chair. Something uncertain niggled at the back of her brain.

"I thought you might have been more comfortable in the guest room, but I hated to wake you up." Mr. Walker stood at the stove in the kitchen and hollered over his shoulder.

"That's okay." She rolled her neck, relieved that the throbbing in her head had quieted to a dull roar.

Mr. Walker handed her a plate with a grilled cheese and some fresh fruit. She accepted it and scooted back on the chair. "Thank you."

He sat down on the couch with a plate of his own. He picked up the remote and turned down the volume on some Sandra Bullock movie. "Grilled cheese is my specialty."

Heather took a bite and her mouth watered. Around a mouthful of sandwich, she said, "This is the best grilled cheese that I've ever had. Ever. Ever." She took another bite, savoring the taste.

Mr. Walker smiled. The resemblance around his eyes to his son was uncanny. "I'm not sure it's that good."

"It is. And I hadn't realized how hungry I was."

"Well, I'm glad." He took a bite of his own sandwich and chewed thoughtfully. "After my wife died, I had to learn to cook. A person gets sick of takeout pretty quick." He stabbed a fresh strawberry with his fork and popped it in his mouth. "Zach tells me you opened a bed-and-breakfast here in Quail Hollow."

"I have. But it's off to a rough start." She cut her gaze to the handsome gentleman. "As I'm sure you're aware, the barn on the property just burned down."

"You'll have time to rebuild once that..." His jaw clenched. "Once Fox is back in custody."

Heather pulled apart her sandwich and stared at the long strand of cheese. "I know. I'm lucky to still be around to do these things." She cleared her throat. "I'm sorry about your daughter."

"You say that as if you somehow feel responsible for my daughter's death."

That same familiar guilt stole her breath. "I knew what Brian was capable of, yet I ran off and hid. I can't help but feel guilty."

Mr. Walker set his plate aside and rested his elbow on the arm of the couch. He stared off into the middle distance and took a deep breath, as if he were about to share a very painful story. Heather considered stopping him. She didn't want to cause the man any more pain, but something deep in her heart suggested he needed to talk. And she needed to hear this.

He ran a hand across his mouth. "For the longest time I blamed myself, too."

Heather's reflex was to tell him, "No, of course it's not your fault," but she knew how that worked. The guilty party never believed it anyway. She set her plate aside and held the blanket close to her chest.

"My wife died when Jill was only sixteen. I was always busy working. Away at a job. And when I was home, I was as strict and tough as when I was on the job. It was the only way I knew how to parent." Other than a quick sniff, Zach's father revealed no sign of emotion. "She met Fox when she was eighteen and they were married six months later." He swallowed hard. Jill's story sounded oddly like hers. Brian knew how to take advantage of vulnerable young women. "I think he was her ticket out of the house. She couldn't wait to get out from under my strict reign."

Heather opened her mouth to offer him some reassurance, as people often did with her. But he held up his hand. "My mind tells me I'm not to blame. That Fox was an evil man. But my heart hurts. If I had been able to provide my daughter with warmth at home, she wouldn't have been so eager to get out of the house. Or…" He turned and met Heather's gaze and something flickered in the depths of his eyes.

"I can only imagine how different our lives would have been if my wife had lived. She and Jill were so close." He drew in a deep breath and let it out. "As you can see, there's enough blame to go around. Zach has his own burden of guilt, but he refuses to talk about it. Our goal has been to see that Fox pays. Control the things we can. Get him behind bars. *Again.*"

"I suppose that's a good strategy. Otherwise you can drive yourself crazy." Heather understood more than most what it was like to feel lost and hopeless. The need to control what little she could.

"Your testimony helped secure Fox's conviction. You did good. Please, never regret your role in this."

Heather nodded, a lump forming in her throat. "I really thought we'd be able to put things behind us once he went to prison."

Mr. Walker picked up his plate and moved the fruit around with his fork. "It'll be over soon. Fox can't run forever."

No, no, he can't.

FOURTEEN

The sun had dipped below the hills. The sky still held a hint of purple. The air had a bite to it. Even if Fox was able to stay on the run where temperatures could plummet well below zero once winter hit, he'd need help if he wanted to survive.

Help. That was what bugged Zach. Earlier, he had talked to his supervisor, who assured him the local authorities still had the woman who provided Fox with the tools to escape prison under tight surveillance as she awaited legal proceedings. They had positively identified the man who they initially thought was Fox through his dental records. He was a high school dropout who liked to spend his time at one of the taverns near the correctional facility. Apparently the dead man had simply been in the wrong place at the wrong time. Fox had either hitched a ride with the man or carjacked him. The ending had been the same: the dead man's car and body ended up in Quail Hollow.

Zach turned the heat on in the truck. He decided to call his boss again, who wholeheartedly supported his decision to remain in Quail Hollow. Yet no one had any updates. Then he called his father. Heather was sleeping and all was quiet at the cabin.

Thank You, Lord. The quick prayer had come naturally and Zach realized Heather had influenced him far more than he had ever imagined. It was easy to turn his back on his faith after Jill was murdered, but now as he turned to prayer, he recalled the comfort that faith could bring in times of crisis. His mother had taught him that, but he had forgotten. Heather had reminded him.

But he realized he couldn't keep Heather safely tucked away. That was why he had to get Fox once and for all. Growing desperate and frustrated, he decided he'd drive the roads of Quail Hollow one more time and see if he noticed anything out of the ordinary.

When he reached the Quail Hollow Bed & Breakfast, he decided to do a property check. All the doors and windows were locked. All appeared secure.

The smell of burned wood still hung in the air. If Zach didn't know better, he'd think someone had been sitting around a campfire. In the gathering darkness, the shell of the barn was a stark reminder of how much worse it could have been if he hadn't raced back here when he had.

He found himself pausing and saying a silent prayer of gratitude. God had truly put him in the right place at the right time to save Heather from certain death.

He strode back around to the driveway, hyperaware of his surroundings. He scanned the area with his flashlight. The light bounced off something metal across the street, partially blocked by the abandoned buggy.

Strange.

With his hand hovering over the grip of his gun, he turned off the flashlight and jogged across the street. When he reached the buggy, he flattened himself against it and moved under cover toward the vehicle that had caught his attention.

His pulse spiked.

His truck. The one that had been stolen.

Exactly where he had parked it the very first night he had arrived at the bed-and-breakfast when Fox escaped. Was this a message? That he had been watching all along?

He scanned his surroundings. No sign of movement. He slid the switch on his flashlight and lifted it to examine the interior of the cab. The beam of light lit on Brian Fox, head tilted back, eyes closed.

Adrenaline surged through his system.

Zach aimed his gun at the one man he hated most in the world. The man who had destroyed so many lives.

Tucking the flashlight under his arm, he yanked open the door and aimed his gun at Fox's head. The temptation to pull the trigger and kill the poor excuse for a human being blackened his heart. His hand trembled on the trigger and a voice whispered in his head, *That's not you. Don't kill him. Take him into custody. He'll be judged by someone far greater than you.*

Swallowing hard, Zach took a step closer and grabbed Fox's arm. A chill ran down his spine. Fox's head lolled over. His body was cool.

Zach checked Fox's pulse. Nothing.

He couldn't have been dead long.

But he *was* dead.

Definitely dead.

Zach holstered his gun and stood frozen for a minute, unsure of how to feel.

"It's all over," he muttered to himself. "It's really over."

He grabbed his phone and called Deputy Gates. "I found Brian Fox. He's dead."

"Where are you?"

"I'm across the street from Quail Hollow Bed & Breakfast."

"I don't understand. We've been patrolling that area."

"Fox was sitting in the driver's seat in my truck. The truck was partially hidden by an abandoned buggy."

"Couldn't have been there long. We've been thorough." He could hear a rustling. "The log says that a patrol was through there fifteen minutes ago."

Zach tapped the side of the truck with the palm of his hand. "Well, he's here now."

"I'll follow up on it. But are you sure it's Brian Fox?"

"Yes, it's definitely him. No gun blast to the face this time." He moved back in front of the open truck door. "I know I hit him when he was making his escape." He turned on his flashlight and saw blood staining his tan T-shirt. "So, either I hit him or someone else did. Either way, the road has ended for Mr. Fox."

Heather rolled over and slowly opened her eyes, surprised at how well she had slept. The bed was very comfortable, especially for a guest room. She pushed up on her elbow, testing to see how much pain she was in. The throbbing in her head had dulled and the bruise on her cheek was tender to the touch. But she'd survive.

She pushed back the hand-sewn quilt that someone—maybe Jill, maybe Jill's mother— had perhaps picked up at an Amish sale. The hardwood floor was cool on her bare feet, reminding her that winter was coming.

She pulled back the room-darkening curtains and stared outside. Clouds cast an eerie glow over the early morning. She reached over and picked up her cell phone on the bedside table— 7:17 a.m.

Unease crawled up her spine as she imagined her enraged ex-husband skulking around the woods, determined to find her after learning that she had escaped the inferno, her certain death.

He had failed at controlling her, once again.

Crossing her arms over her oversize T-shirt, she turned away from the window. Curiosity had her moving toward her bedroom door. Surely Zach had returned sometime last night. Did he have news?

She paused at the mirror and smiled. She better take a few minutes to get presentable before she checked to see if her host was awake.

After she got dressed, she went to the kitchen. Zach and his father sat at the kitchen table drinking coffee. Mr. Walker looked up and smiled. He pushed away from the table and the back of his chair hit the door leading out to the backyard. "Good morning." He lifted his mug and took a sip, then set it down. "Okay, what kind of eggs would everyone like? I'll get the bacon on."

Heather narrowed her gaze. An entirely different mood settled, albeit subtly, into the cozy space, as if a weight had been lifted. Had something happened last night?

Zach stood and pulled out a chair for Heather. "Sit down. My father wouldn't allow us to help, even if we asked. What kind of eggs would you like?"

Heather lifted her hands, not wanting to be an imposition. "Whatever's easiest."

Mr. Walker grabbed the eggs from the fridge and spun around to face them. "Why don't I make a big batch of scrambled eggs?"

Heather's stomach grumbled. "Sounds good."

Zach grabbed a mug and the coffeepot. He set the mug in front of her and smiled. "Cream and sugar are right here."

"Thank you." She traced the handle of the plain ceramic mug, then met Zach's gaze. She almost hated to ask because she feared the answer, but she couldn't delay any longer. "Any word on the search?"

If she hadn't looked up from the sugar bowl, she might have missed the quick exchange between father and son. Her heart plummeted. "Do you have news?"

Zach let out a long breath. "Yes, I do." He seemed to be searching for the right words. Goose bumps blanketed her skin as she anticipated his update.

"Did Brian hurt someone else?" She swallowed around a knot of emotion.

Zach pressed his lips together, then reached across the table to cover her hand. His hand felt warm on hers. Comforting.

"What is it?" she whispered.

"Last night I was searching your property—"

"At the bed-and-breakfast?" She couldn't keep the tremble out of her voice.

"Yes. I found my stolen truck parked across the street with Fox at the wheel. He was dead."

Heather's hand flew to her chest as a flush of an emotion she couldn't quite pinpoint settled on her lungs, making it difficult to breathe. "Brian's dead?" She lifted her watery gaze to him. "Are you sure?"

Zach squeezed her hand. "Yes. I saw the body myself. There's no mistake this time."

She nodded slowly, as if in a fog. "It's over. It's really over."

"Yes. It's over. I wanted to tell you last night, but you were sleeping so peacefully I didn't want to wake you."

"How did he die?"

"Best guess? He succumbed to the wound when I shot him," Zach said. "I checked with the sheriff's department that he had been shot, apparently twice. An autopsy will confirm cause of death."

Heather pulled her hand out from under his and placed each of her hands on either side of her coffee mug, focusing on the warmth flowing off the ceramic. A tear trailed down her cheek.

Zach brushed the tear away. "I'm sorry you've had to go through all this."

Heather nodded again, trying to let the news settle in. "I can go back to the bed-and-breakfast. Get back to my life." She tilted her head toward him and winced at the pain. "I suppose you'll be getting back to Buffalo, too."

Zach smiled but didn't say anything. Heather didn't know what to make of it.

Heather felt a gentle hand on her shoulder. She glanced up into Mr. Walker's kind eyes. "Everything's going to be okay."

Heather's lips trembled. This man had lost

his beautiful daughter and he was comforting her. She reached up and patted his hand. "Thank you for keeping me company last night. It meant a lot to me."

"It was my pleasure." He grabbed the pan of eggs from the stove and dished them out. He set three plates down on the table. "I can understand why my son talks so highly of you."

Zach cleared his throat. "We're not telling tales out of school, are we?"

Mr. Walker picked up a piece of bacon with his fingers. "I like to be helpful. My son here would be all work and no play…"

Zach laughed. "I'm a grown man. I think I can get my own dates."

Heather felt her face heat as she moved the eggs around her plate with the fork.

Zach took a sip of his coffee, then set it back down. "Can we just eat and enjoy the peace? We finally don't have anything to worry about."

Nothing to worry about.

Heather's mind flashed to the barn and her canceled reservations at the bed-and-breakfast. She had a lot to take care of—a lot to worry about—but God had seen to it that her biggest concern was no longer a threat.

She scooped up the eggs and couldn't believe how delicious they were. "These are fantastic. I'm not going to be in a hurry to go anywhere." Then realizing what she'd said, she quickly backtracked. "I mean…"

Both Walker men laughed. "We know what you mean," Zach said as he bit into a piece of bacon. "My father really knows how to cook."

Shortly after breakfast, Zach had plans to drive Heather home to the bed-and-breakfast. "You're welcome to stay at the cabin for a few more days to recover. My father loves cooking for you."

Heather tugged on her seat belt, seeming anxious. "As wonderful as that sounds, I need to get home. To start figuring out what I need to do to have the burned-out barn replaced. I need to reassure those who have future reservations that we'll be reopening for business soon. I can't afford to waste any more time. This is peak tourist season. Once winter arrives, business will slow down, maybe even come to a halt." She dragged a hand through her hair and sighed heavily, sounding weary. "And I can't put you and your father out any longer."

"Don't overdo it. Promise me? You've had a concussion." He wanted to say so much more, but now didn't seem like the right time. He didn't want to pressure her.

"I'll try." He knew it would be a struggle

considering how determined she was to make a success of the bed-and-breakfast.

"I have to get back to Buffalo for work, but I could come back on the weekends and help you with projects."

Heather shifted in her seat but didn't say anything. For the first time in a long time, Zach felt an air of awkwardness stretch between them. Something that hadn't existed between them before. Perhaps he had said too much.

Zach cleared his throat, wanting to backtrack. "I figured you could use some help."

"I really could, but you have a life, a job, in Buffalo. I don't want to take advantage of your kindness. You've already done so much."

Zach knew a brush-off when he heard it, but he also realized Heather had been through an awful lot recently and it wasn't fair of him to expect her to make any other plans for the future other than getting her bed-and-breakfast up and running.

He slowed and turned into her driveway. His vehicle bobbled over the ruts created by the hardened mud. Sloppy Sam—Zach couldn't help but smile inside every time he thought of the workman's nickname—was installing a handmade sign on the front lawn: Quail Hollow Bed & Breakfast.

"Look at that," Heather said, an air of excite-

ment in her voice. "The sign looks beautiful."
She climbed out of his vehicle and went over
to chat with the Amish workman.

Zach parked and got out. He grabbed her
overnight bag from the backseat and slung the
strap over his shoulder. "Where do you want
me to put this?"

"I'll take it." Heather held out her hand. "I
don't want to hold you up."

"No, you need to take it easy. I'll carry your
bag in and put it on the landing upstairs."

Heather smiled, a genuine smile. The weight
of recent events seemed to have lifted and left a
light in her eyes. "I won't argue. Upstairs would
be great." She turned to Sam. "Thank you. The
sign looks awesome." She traced the carved let-
tering with her index finger. "Just beautiful."

Sam tipped his broad-brimmed hat. *"Denki."*

Heather jogged and caught up with Zach. She
slipped ahead of him and reached out to unlock
the door to the house, when it swung open. She
glanced back at him with a startled expression.

Was someone inside?

Zach was about to stop Heather's entry when
Ruthie's voice rang out. "You're home!" Heather's shoulders relaxed at her friend's greeting.

"I am." Heather stepped aside to hold the
door open, allowing Zach to pass.

"I'll run this upstairs." Zach patted her bag

and jogged up the stairs. When he came back down, Heather was sitting at the table in the new addition while Ruthie put the kettle on.

"Stay for some tea, Marshal Walker?" There was something very hopeful, almost gleeful, in her tone.

"I should probably go."

"Don't run off. Not yet." Heather glanced at the seat next to hers. "Sit down a minute."

He sat down at the table, not eager to leave. "Our view isn't quite the same as it was a few days ago." In the bright sunshine, the loss of the barn was staggering. Heather seemed to stare at it for a long moment, as if reflecting on how she had almost lost her life in the raging fire.

Ruthie set out two cups of tea and a few cookies. "I'm going to run upstairs and do some cleaning." She paused in the doorway. "Thanks for keeping my *gut* friend safe."

Heather pushed the plate of cookies toward Zach and he waved them off and she laughed in response. "Yeah, I'm not exactly hungry, either. Not after that breakfast your father made us."

They sat in silence for a few minutes, sipping their tea. After a stretch, Zach stood up. "I guess I shouldn't prolong the inevitable." It seemed they were playing a game of who was going to say goodbye first.

Heather stood up, joining him. She placed

her hand on his chest and leaned up on her tippy-toes and kissed his cheek. "I'll miss you."

Zach tilted his head back and smiled. "You know where to find me if you need a hand around here."

"Be careful what you offer."

"I wouldn't offer to help if I didn't mean it."

Zach cupped her soft cheek, then let his hand drop. He turned to leave before he changed his mind.

FIFTEEN

A few days had passed and Heather was feeling much better. The only outward sign of her injuries was a slight yellowish mark under her eye. Nothing a little makeup wouldn't cover up.

On her trip to the grocery store, the sun seemed brighter and the air smelled sweeter. She had said more than her share of prayers for Brian's soul, but now was her time to move on. Thank God that He had protected her and those she cared about.

Picking out the groceries for this weekend's guests had been a pure pleasure. The bed-and-breakfast had been aired out and was ready for guests. She could finally get on with her life without constantly looking over her shoulder.

As she wandered the aisles, her mind drifted to Zach. She missed him. He had called yesterday to check in on her, but the conversation had been brief. Perhaps neither one of them knew what to say after all they had been through.

His presence here had been part of his job. *That's all.*

He owed her nothing more. Her feelings for him were born out of gratitude. *That's all.*

Heather smiled at the cashier as she paid, then loaded the groceries into her car to head home. She thought of her mother as she drove. Apparently her mind wouldn't allow her to have a completely worry-free day. She supposed it was her nature. Her mother's murder had never been solved, but maybe it was time to put her mind at peace and focus on the fact that her mom wasn't suffering. She was in heaven. She wouldn't want her eldest daughter to waste any more of her life trying to uncover the evil of the past.

Even though Heather wasn't Amish, she needed to follow the Amish way in honor of her mother and forgive the murderer. Move on.

Brian was gone, that was the most important thing. That part of her past was over. She was safe.

Maybe it *was* time to let it all rest.

A car's horn honked behind her. She glanced into her rearview mirror and muttered, "Sorry," even though he couldn't hear her. She wasn't sure how long she had been sitting at the stop sign. She looked both ways and moved through the intersection.

The car behind her sped up and zipped around her. Heather cringed when she noticed a horse and buggy traveling on the shoulder in the opposite direction. The Amish woman frowned and pulled up on the reins when the car sped past.

It seemed the tranquility the Amish sought was forever being encroached upon by the *Englischers*. Heather wondered if she was respecting her grandmother's home by allowing outsiders in.

Her worries fell away when she arrived home and saw the beautiful sign Sloppy Sam had constructed on the front lawn: Quail Hollow Bed & Breakfast. She had to believe her *mammy* was happy to have family back in her home.

Her proud feelings were replaced by curiosity when she noticed a car parked in the driveway. She wasn't expecting guests. "Is that Fiona's car?" she muttered to herself. Had the writer shown up unannounced? Heather didn't think she was scheduled to stay. Maybe Ruthie had taken the reservation and forgot to mention it. Yet they didn't take reservations for a weekday.

Heather popped the trunk and grabbed a few of the grocery bags. She'd return for the rest in a few minutes.

When she climbed the steps to the porch, she heard loud voices coming from inside. She set the bags down on the porch and opened the door. Nerves tangled inside her stomach.

Fiona stood with her back to the door. Ruthie was begging Fiona to leave. From her vantage point, Heather couldn't see Fiona's face to get a better read on the situation.

"What's going on?" Heather asked, her mouth growing dry as her nerves buzzed.

Fiona spun around, her face radiating rage. Reflexively, Heather recoiled; her instincts told her to get away. The same instincts that had convinced her it had been time to leave her husband.

Confusion swirled in her brain.

"What's going on?" she repeated when no one answered her.

"Run," Ruthie yelled. The fear in her friend's voice struck terror in Heather's heart.

Fiona slowly pulled her hand out of her jacket pocket and pointed a gun at Heather's chest. "Run and either you or your Amish friend here dies."

Heather slowly lifted her hands in a surrender gesture. "No one needs to get hurt. Please, lower the gun."

What in the world was going on?

Fiona shook her head slowly. "No." Her

clipped answer made Heather's stomach bottom out.

"I don't understand," Heather said as her vision tunneled onto Fiona's face. The determination in her eyes behind her thick glasses landed squarely on Heather.

"I tried to get her to leave, but she threatened me," Ruthie said apologetically. "She insisted on seeing you. I'm sorry. So sorry." Her voice trembled.

"It's okay, Ruthie. It's okay."

Fiona stepped closer to Heather and the smell of beer wafted off her breath. "What do you want, Fiona?"

"You."

The single word made her knees go weak. "I'm sorry. What?"

"You… I want you dead." Fiona flashed the gun as if it were no big deal.

"I don't understand. What have I ever done to you?" Despite insides of mush, Heather projected a commanding tone.

"Please, Fiona, don't hurt Heather," Ruthie said, on the verge of tears. "She's like a sister to me. Please."

Fiona's eyes darted around the room, as if she was trying to weigh her options. She grabbed Heather's arm and squeezed tightly. Heather didn't react. She had had a lot of experience in tamping down her reaction when Brian was raging. He'd fed off her fear and she'd refused to give him more fuel for his anger.

"Amish girl, sit down and shut up."

Ruthie lowered herself into a chair at the kitchen table and clasped her hands in front of her. All the color had drained from her face.

"It's okay," Heather reassured her. "Everything's going to be okay."

Ruthie bowed her bonneted head. A sob escaped her lips.

Heather's stomach twisted.

Fiona leaned in close to Heather and clenched her teeth. "I need a second to think."

Zach sat at his desk at the downtown Buffalo U.S. Marshals office. This was the part of the job he liked least: paperwork. And nothing created more paperwork than a dead escaped convict. He wouldn't be able to wrap up the case until Fox's autopsy was complete. He moved the mouse and the computer screen came to life. He had just entered his log-in and password when he heard a soft knock on the door.

He hit the enter key, then turned halfheartedly toward the door, expecting one of his colleagues, eager to hear about the big manhunt that had transfixed the state over the past few weeks. What he hadn't expected was his father, dressed casually in a golf shirt and jeans.

Zach removed his hand from the computer mouse and leaned back in his chair. "Hey, Dad."

"You look as excited about that paperwork as I used to feel." His father crossed his arms and gave him an easy smile.

"I don't suppose the paperwork is why any of us got into law enforcement."

"But it might be the reason we retire." His father sat down in the chair on the other side of the desk and crossed his ankle over his knee.

"What brings you by?" Zach knew his father liked to catch up with his former colleagues now and again, but he usually gave his son a quick text letting him know he'd be in.

"I can't stop by and say hello to my son?"

Zach eyed his father skeptically. Theirs was a solid relationship, but not a touchy-feely one. "Sure you can. I'm glad you stopped by. I was hoping to take you out to dinner this week. Thank you for your help in Quail Hollow."

"No need to repay me with dinner. I was glad to help." His dad rubbed his hands up and down his thighs. "An old guy like me likes to feel useful now and again."

"Well, I appreciate it."

"Speaking of Quail Hollow, are you going to keep in touch with Heather Miller?" His father dropped his foot to the floor and leveled his gaze at his son.

Zach frowned and lifted his hand in a casual gesture, as if it were of no consequence.

"Life goes by too fast. You've been all about this job for a long time. You need to let someone in." His father tapped the edge of the desk with his fingers for emphasis.

"You know what the job's like."

"I do." His father sat back in his chair. "And I loved the job like you do. But what I wouldn't do to be able to go back and spend more time with your mother. I'd trade anything for it. Now I'm retired. And all alone."

Zach was about to tell his father that he had him, but he knew that wasn't what his father meant. His father had spent most of his adult life chasing criminals. Then he lost his wife too soon. Then, tragically, he lost his daughter...

Zach cleared his throat. "Heather and I are clearly on two different paths."

"But perhaps God brought your paths together for a reason."

Out of the corner of his eye, he noticed his computer screen went blank. In the past, any mention of church, God or faith had made Zach bristle. But this time it hadn't. Heather's doing, most likely.

"Perhaps you're right." Zach raised his eyebrows. "Not really sure what I'm supposed to do about it. I don't want to crowd her. She's been through a lot. She needs time." Out of habit, he reached over and wiggled the mouse and the screen came to life.

"Well, I'll let you get to your paperwork." His father stood and paused in the doorway. "But don't give her too much time. She might meet herself a nice Amish guy."

"You don't have to do this," Heather said as she took a chance and backed away from Fiona in the small kitchen of the bed-and-breakfast, hoping—praying—she could find something to defend herself with.

Fiona wore a blank expression that unnerved Heather more than the fuming she was doing earlier. She seemed disconnected, catatonic. "You really don't get it, do you?" Her tone was flat.

Heather swallowed hard. "Get what?"

"It doesn't surprise me. He said you were a stupid woman."

Heather's heart plummeted and nausea roiled in her gut as she took another step back and reached behind her to feel for the drawer where she kept the knives.

He...he...he...

Heather knew exactly who *he* was. She felt

it in her bones. Brian Fox had manipulated another impressionable young woman.

Even in death, he was coming back to mess with her life.

The room grew close. Too close. A bead of sweat rolled down her back. She had to keep talking to distract Fiona. Distract herself from her rioting thoughts. "Who are you talking about?" Despite her best efforts, Heather's voice cracked. She needed Fiona to say it. To confirm what Heather already suspected.

Don't show your fear.

"He was obsessed with you. Even after everything I did for him, he still wanted you." Fiona's eyes narrowed into slits behind her glasses.

A buzzing hummed in Heather's ears and the ground shifted beneath her.

"*You* helped my ex-husband escape prison?" How could that be? Zach said they had already arrested someone and she was out on bail.

Fiona rolled her eyes, mocking her. "No, of course not. How would I do that? That other stupid woman who worked at the correctional facility helped him. He was just using her. Besides, she was stupid. She deserved to get caught."

Brian was charismatic. He knew how to charm women. Even in prison he had charmed multiple women into helping him. How had he reached Fiona?

Keep Fiona talking.

Heather's fingers brushed across a smooth drawer handle. Inside were several serrated knives. Could she open it without drawing Fiona's attention?

Bigger question: Could she use a knife on another human being?

"How did you know Brian?" Heather scanned the room behind Fiona, calculating how difficult it would be to shove her out of the way and make her escape. But even if she could, Ruthie might not.

"I wrote him in prison because I wanted to write his story. *His* side of the story."

"Brian beat me. He killed his second wife. What more did you need to know?"

"That's *your* side of the story. He needed to be able to tell his."

A throbbing started behind Heather's eyes. "Brian's dead. Why are you doing this now?"

"You're the reason he's dead."

Heather's pulse whooshed in her ears.

"He said he'd be with me when he got out. But he was obsessed with you." Fiona turned her head and stared out the kitchen window toward the burned-out barn. A small smile played at the corners of her mouth.

Realization smothered Heather like a too-heavy itchy blanket on a hot summer's day. She struggled to catch her breath. This woman was completely irrational. "You tried to kill me in the barn. You were the one who slammed the bag over my head and started the fire."

"I didn't want you to see me. I wanted you to die thinking the man you tossed aside had killed you."

"But why?" Heather swallowed hard, trying to tamp down her panic.

"I thought he wouldn't be with me until you were out of the picture. As long as you were alive, Brian would prefer you to me."

Heather tried to keep her breath even. "Brian's gone now. He can't be with anyone." She held her breath, watching Fiona's face flush red. Had she said too much? "What do you expect to gain now?"

"A little satisfaction."

"I don't understand." Heather's limbs trembled, fully realizing she was carrying on a discussion with someone who had discarded logic for some sort of warped revenge.

"He's dead because of you." This conversation was going in circles.

Pinpricks blanketed her scalp and she swallowed back her fear. "I didn't kill him."

Fiona turned and glared at Heather as if she

had offended her. "Can you believe he got mad at me after he found out I tried to kill you in the barn fire? I thought he'd be happy that I had gone after the woman who put him in jail. But he told me I had no right. He told me he was still committed to you. That he had left you your wedding ring. Is that true?"

Ruthie gasped, but Heather kept her attention on the woman in front of her. "Yes," Heather said, afraid to lie. "He left it in the medicine cabinet. But I didn't want anything to do with Brian. I was done with him."

Fiona flinched, as if the words hurt, or perhaps confused her. "Brian was every bit as controlling as you said he was. But I thought if you were out of the way, we could be together." Her voice held a faraway quality. "But I was wrong."

"He's gone now. It's over. He can't hurt either one of us anymore. Don't you see that?"

"It won't be over until you're gone, too. Because of you, I couldn't have Brian. You destroyed everything. You need to pay."

"Fiona, think about what you're doing. You'll go to prison. You'll have let Brian destroy your life, too."

"It's already destroyed." Fiona lifted her hands to her temples, still holding the gun.

"Tell me how he died." Heather tried to distract her.

Fiona's lips began to tremble and she lowered her hands. "He was already nursing a bullet wound to the arm—the jerk was wearing a bulletproof vest when your boyfriend shot at him as he tried to get away on the boat."

Heather reached behind her and inched the drawer open a fraction as Fiona unraveled her story, seeming to revel in the details. Maybe she still planned to write this story.

Fiona continued, "But once I realized he had used me to get to you, I decided to put another bullet in him. End it for him. I waited until he was good and dead, then I left him in the truck across the street. It was all so neat. I had a perfect ending to my story. The bad guy gets his comeuppance." Fiona's finger twitched near the trigger, sending renewed unease twisting up Heather's spine. Fiona looked off into the distance, as if she was plotting something. "Heather Miller's ex-husband is found dead in her boyfriend's stolen truck. Readers love those kind of twists."

Fiona had gone over the edge. Heather had long ceased talking to a sane person, but she had to try if she hoped to get out of here alive with Ruthie. "No one would have ever known about your involvement. Coming here today couldn't be worth jeopardizing your freedom. Could it?" Heather held her breath, waiting for her answer.

"The story wasn't complete. Brian was supposed to be with me. I was going to write his *complete* story, which was supposed to end with me and him together. But he couldn't be with me because he was obsessed with you. He was always going to be obsessed with you. You ruined my happy ending." Her eyebrows rose in an awkward gesture, then her gaze lowered to her shaking hand holding the gun.

"It's not too late to walk away," Heather pleaded. "You can claim self-defense with Brian. And you haven't hurt me or Ruthie. You can walk away," she repeated, maintaining eye contact with her captor. The light from over the sink glinted off her glasses. "You can be the hero of your story."

Behind her, Heather eased the drawer open just a little bit more. She slid her fingers in and felt for the handle of a knife. Pinching it awkwardly with her fingers, she eased the knife out of the tray. It hit the edge of the drawer and clattered back down on top of the other silverware.

Fiona's eyes flared wide. She stepped back, kicked the drawer shut, lifted the gun and aimed it at Heather's heart. "Yes, I *am* going to write the ending. *My* way."

SIXTEEN

Heather held up her hands, trying to appease Fiona. Trying to make her forget she had just been caught trying to slide a knife out of the utensil drawer. "Please don't do this." She hated the squeak in her voice.

Ruthie cried quietly in the corner.

Heather would never be able to overpower a deranged woman with a gun, so her only chance was to talk her way out of this. Dread tightened like a band around her lungs. She hadn't been able to make any headway so far, but she had to keep trying.

"You're a writer. You want a great story? Why don't you write about my mother's murder?" Shame in the form of heat swept up Heather's cheeks. *Please forgive me, Lord, for using my mother's tragedy like this.*

Fiona lowered her gun a fraction, as if considering.

"I can give you my side of the story. How I

grew up Amish and my father left the Amish community heartbroken after my mother was murdered."

"I told you that would make a great story. I'd probably become famous." Intrigue softened Fiona's tone.

"Yes, it's a story that needs to be told."

Fiona lifted an eyebrow, skepticism lining her eyes.

"Doesn't everyone like a good mystery?" Heather hated herself for using her mother like this.

"But, you told me you valued your privacy. You made me feel like a loser for being gossipy with your other houseguests." Fiona frowned, as if considering something. "I don't like being made to feel bad about myself. I would have just continued to spy from the barn without your criticism, but I couldn't get close enough."

"That was you?" Heather's hand flew to her mouth. *Of course.* The police had been checking the restaurant surveillance cameras for possible images of Brian. Fiona could have easily slipped in unnoticed between the cheerleaders who had been there at the same time.

"People have been underestimating me my entire life. I found a ladder behind the barn. Realized I could spy on you from the loft." Fiona hiked up her chin, obviously proud of herself. "About your mother's murder…"

Trying her best to sound calm despite having a gun aimed at her, Heather said, "I've had time to think about it since we first talked. My mother's story needs to be told. Maybe your book will lead the police to her killer."

Something flitted in the depths of Fiona's eyes. "Exactly. That's why I started writing true crime. The victim's story needs to be told."

"You were never writing a romance?" Heather wasn't sure why she even asked, perhaps just to keep Fiona talking.

Her captor shrugged. "I dabble. But true crime is my passion."

"But why did you want to tell Brian's story and not Jill's? He wasn't the victim."

Fiona froze and her nostrils flared. "Sometimes the story the media portrays isn't the truth."

"My mother and Heather's mother were best friends when Mrs. Miller disappeared," Ruthie said in a soft, frightened voice from her chair in the corner.

Heather's heart stopped, uncertain what Fiona would do with that information. Heather never had any intention of sharing her mother's story—not with Fiona, anyway—she was just trying to talk her way out of this situation. Buy some time.

Fiona turned slowly to look at Ruthie. "Is that so?"

Ruthie's eyes grew wide. She nodded.

Fiona spun around and grabbed Heather's ponytail and pushed her toward the front door. She pressed the gun into her spine. "Get up," she yelled at Ruthie. "We're leaving." Ruthie jumped up and knocked over the chair.

Heather's scalp ached as Fiona shoved her outside, down the stairs and toward her car. Ruthie followed behind.

"Where are we going?" Heather asked.

"We have to get out of here. I know. I watched this place for a long time. Workers might be here soon." Fiona's gaze darted around. Her grip tightened on Heather's ponytail. "Besides—" her tone grew curious "—I want to meet Ruthie's mom now."

Fiona reached into her pocket and pulled out the keys and opened the trunk.

A weight pressed down on Heather's chest and she could already feel the suffocating heat and closeness of the trunk. "Please, please, *please*, don't do this." She made eye contact ever so briefly with a terrified Ruthie.

"Get in the trunk or I'll kill you and your very helpful friend." Fiona shrugged, as if taunting her. "Ruthie gets to ride up front and give me directions to her mom's house."

Ruthie looked like she was about to pass out.

Realizing she had no option, Heather lifted a shaky leg and stepped into the trunk. Just as she was debating how she could gracefully climb into the space to become Fiona's hostage, her kidnapper planted both hands on Heather's back and shoved her in. She landed heavily on a partially sunken spare tire, some half-empty water bottles and a pair of tennis shoes.

Before she had a chance to make one last plea, Fiona slammed the trunk shut, leaving her to suck in stale carpet fumes.

Heather could hear muffled voices as Fiona undoubtedly threatened Ruthie at gunpoint to comply. Car doors slammed. The engine started. Desperation and exhaust fumes made Heather dizzy, yet she pushed with all her might on the trunk lid. It didn't budge. Heather didn't know a lot about cars, but she suspected this old beater was manufactured before safety experts put releases inside the trunk.

Panic made it difficult to think. *Breathe. In through the nose, hold for three, out through the mouth.*

Dear Lord, help me. Help me and Ruthie.

The cell phone sitting on the corner of Zach's desk vibrated. He considered letting it go to voice mail as he tried to catch up on a mountain of work, but something made him pick it up.

"Marshal Walker?" came the breathless voice over the phone line. "This is Sloppy Sam."

Zach pushed back in his chair and it bounced off the wall as he stood. Dread coursed through him. "What's wrong?"

"Are you still in Quail Hollow?"

"No, I'm back at my office in Buffalo. What's going on?"

"I showed up at the bed-and-breakfast to tie up a few loose ends and the back door was open and a kitchen chair was knocked over. Miss Miller's trunk was open with groceries inside. Seemed like someone left in a hurry. I wanted to make sure Miss Miller was okay. I thought if you were still in town, maybe she was with you."

"No, she's not." Heart beating wildly in his chest, he swallowed hard. "I need you to hang up and call the sheriff immediately. Tell him what you just told me."

"*Yah*, I will." Sloppy Sam ended the call.

Zach stared at his phone as panic crashed into him. He drew in a deep breath, knowing he had to keep calm. He dialed Heather's number and waited. Her cheerful voice sounded on the voice mail. He waited and left a message.

"I need to make sure you're okay. Call me as soon as you get this message. Thanks."

Zach pushed back his chair and snagged his jacket from the coatrack in the corner of his office. Shoving his arms into his jacket, he ran to the elevator. He found himself praying for Heather's safety.

He had to get to Quail Hollow. Make sure she was okay.

When he got down to the parking lot and into his brand-new truck, he called Deputy Gates to make sure Sam had called it in. At least now Zach knew someone local was looking into it.

"Call me if you get any leads. I'm leaving from Buffalo for Quail Hollow now. I should be there in an hour."

"We'll find out what's going on," the deputy reassured him.

As Zach tore out of the parking lot, he couldn't imagine what had happened. He had thought the danger had passed once Fox was found dead.

He slowed at a red light, then pounded on the steering wheel. "Come on. Come on. Come on." He glanced both ways, and once it was clear, he blew through the light.

Fiona hadn't driven far when the car bobbled over an uneven road, making every contact point between Heather's body and the trunk of the car ache.

The car came to a stop. Heather strained to listen over her heavy breathing. She knew the trunk wasn't airtight, but the darkness and the stale smell did nothing to alleviate her fears.

The engine cut off. A door slammed. Footsteps.

Please open the trunk. Please open the trunk. Please open the truck.

Anxiety made her heart race.

The footsteps grew more distant and Heather nearly cried when she was abandoned in the trunk with something sharp digging into her side.

Help me, dear Lord. Help me.

Heather wasn't sure how much time had passed when she heard voices. One was Fiona's. Her pulse spiked when she recognized the other: Maryann's.

Where was Ruthie?

"We don't have many plants left. Our peak season is in the spring. All the mums are picked over," Maryann said.

"That's okay." Fiona's voice grew closer. "I had something else in mind."

"Oh…" Maryann sounded confused, but not frightened.

Please leave her out of this. Please, please…

The sound of metal scraping—a key inserted into the trunk lock—didn't provide the sweet relief she had hoped for. Instead she feared for what Fiona would do to Maryann once she saw Heather in the trunk. She'd be a witness who needed to be eliminated.

The crack of light grew larger. The first thing Heather saw was Maryann's horrified face. The Amish woman covered her mouth with her hands. "Heather..."

Ruthie stood nearby. Terror making her mute.

"Ah, yes, sweet Heather. Not exactly what you were expecting." Fiona was talking to Maryann, but she had a gun trained on Heather.

"Oh, my. What's going on?" Maryann backed up and hit her heel on the door of the greenhouse. She turned to her daughter. "Ruthie, what's going on?"

"I'm sorry, *Mem*" was all she could say.

Heather blinked against the bright light after being held in the darkness of the trunk. Fiona had pulled the car around to the back of the greenhouse, where it would be hidden from those searching for it from the street. *If* anyone was searching for it.

Ruthie stood clasping her hands with silent tears falling down her cheeks.

"Leave Maryann out of this," Heather said,

fully realizing she wasn't in a position to make demands.

Immediately Heather figured she had said the wrong thing. Fiona would do exactly the opposite of what Heather wanted her to do.

"I need Maryann for my story. You know, the one you promised me about your mother."

Maryann's brow furrowed as she struggled to comprehend the situation.

"Get out." Fiona pointed the gun at Heather. "And you two," she said to Maryann and Ruthie, "don't go anywhere."

Heather braced her hands on the edge of the trunk and dragged herself out. The ground beneath her swayed. Her feet tingled from the awkward position she had been forced to take in the trunk. She blinked, trying to orient herself. Despite the overcast day, going from the black of the trunk to the light of day felt like tiny pinpricks in her eyes.

"Quit *rutsching*," Fiona said when Heather tried to squirm out of reach. "Did I say that right? Quit squirming, right? I figure if I can sprinkle some Pennsylvania Dutch throughout the book it will make it more authentic. I hear Amish books are big sellers. I had done a little research before coming to Quail Hollow, but I never realized it would come in handy so soon."

"I can help you with that," Heather said in

a desperate attempt to appeal to this crazed young woman. "I spoke Pennsylvania Dutch for the first six years of my life. You don't need them."

Fiona gave her a strange look. "Get inside. All of you." Maryann started walking toward the front of the house when Fiona yelled, "No, the back door."

Maryann led the way, then Ruthie, Heather, followed by a gun-toting Fiona.

Fiona made them sit down at the kitchen table. "If anyone thinks they're going to be a hero, I'll shoot Maryann first." She frowned, a feigned sympathetic gesture that came off as garish. "You all can't get away."

Fiona reached into the bag strapped over her shoulder and pulled out a yellow legal pad. "I prefer to work on my laptop, but I know electricity can be scarce out here." Her words held an air of disgust.

Fiona threw the legal pad on the table. "I wish I had more time to prepare for this interview, but I'm good at working on the fly." She sounded almost gleeful. "Answer the questions honestly." She lifted her eyebrows. "And don't worry. You can help one another if you don't know the answers."

"You can't expect us to answer questions under duress." Heather pushed back from the table. "Why don't you put the gun away and we can chat calmly?"

Fiona aimed the gun at Heather. "You're trying to trick me."

Heather squared her shoulders. She was tired of dealing with bullies. "You can't expect us to answer questions while you're pointing a gun at us." She stood and kept moving so that Fiona had to turn away from Maryann and Ruthie. Fiona's rage grew as she tracked a defiant Heather into the front room. Heather had counted on it. She glanced over Fiona's shoulder at her dear Amish friends. She gave them a subtle nod and mouthed the word *run*.

In her attempt to flee, Maryann knocked Heather's chair over and it bounced off the floor.

Fiona spun around. Heather grabbed a glass pitcher off a shelf and brought it down over Fiona's head. The woman crumpled to the floor and her gun clattered across the hardwood.

Blood pulsing in her ears, Heather stepped over Fiona to grab the gun. At the same time she yelled to Maryann and Ruthie, "Run! Get out!" When Ruthie paused, Heather yelled, "Go, *now*! Call for help."

The Amish woman she had grown to love like a mother moved toward the door, her long skirt fluttering around her legs. Ruthie followed. Heather bent for the gun when Fiona dived at her legs, taking her down. Heather landed on her shoulder with an *oomph*. Twisting, she stretched for the gun while Fiona clawed at her legs.

The tips of Heather's fingers brushed against the cool metal.

A scream tore from Fiona's throat as Heather stretched with everything she had to gain control of the gun. If she didn't get the gun, Fiona would kill her for sure.

SEVENTEEN

The closer Zach got to Quail Hollow Bed & Breakfast, the more fried his nerves became. Deputy Gates had promised he'd call once Heather was located. The silence of his cell phone was unnerving.

He just passed the location where the body had been pulled from the woods behind the Hershbergers' place. The trees dotting the hillside were in peak fall colors. Evil had touched even this beautiful place.

Dear Lord, please help me get to Heather in time.

He didn't know what had happened to Heather, but every ounce of his being knew it was bad.

An image of his sweet sister came to mind.

Let me be there for Heather. Please. I can't let her down, too.

The cell phone on the seat next to him rang, startling him. He had waited the entire drive for it to ring, and now that it had, he was afraid to answer. He had dealt with hundreds of life-and-death situations in his job and now he was truly afraid. Afraid that he may have lost Heather forever.

Drawing in a fortifying breath, he pressed the accept button. "Marshal Walker," he said into the air with his phone set on hands-free.

"It's Deputy Gates…" A determined voice filled the cab of the truck. He bolted upright and his seat belt snapped against his chest.

"You found Heather."

"A call came in from the Hershbergers' residence, Maryann and Ruthie are hiding in the barn. Someone is holding Miss Miller at gunpoint in the main house," he said in clipped tones. "We're headed there now."

Zach slammed on the brakes. "I'm a minute away."

"Wait for backup," the deputy said. "We're en route."

"Okay." Zach ended the call and pressed the accelerator and did a quick U-turn and headed back toward the Hershbergers' farm. He wasn't going to wait for anyone. Not if it meant saving Heather's life.

Zach pulled over about a hundred feet from the handmade wooden sign by the road that read Greenhouse. Apparently the Amish were on the nose in their advertising. The cornfields from the neighboring property would hide the truck. Provide him with the element of surprise.

Zach climbed out and closed the door with a quiet click. He pulled his gun out of its holster and ran toward the driveway, his heart in his throat. When he reached the end of the cornfields, he paused and peered up toward the house.

According to the deputy, Heather was being held captive in the main house. He scanned the windows and didn't notice any movement. He broke away from his hiding place and sprinted toward the house. He took cover by the side of the building, catching his breath.

He listened. He could hear rustling from inside, then a crash. Shouting.

Time was running out to save Heather. Crouching, so as not to be seen from the windows, he moved toward the porch and silently climbed the steps and prayed for backup.

When Heather couldn't reach the gun, she twisted her body around, despite Fiona clawing at her legs. Heather freed her legs and kicked Fiona as hard as she could. Her shoe made solid contact and a horrifying crack came from Fiona's jaw as she fell backward and let out a whoosh of air. Heather scrambled and reached for a table to pull herself up.

"I'm going to kill you," Fiona screamed.

The front door burst open and Zach stepped in, training his gun on Fiona. "Stop."

Relief washed over Heather. *"Zach,"* she breathed.

Before Fiona had a chance to get her legs under her, Zach strode across the room. He shoved his gun back into its holster and quickly put handcuffs on Fiona. "Stay put."

Zach turned and reached for Heather's hand, pulling her toward him. He cupped her cheek with his hand and smoothed his thumb across her skin, leaving a trail of warmth. "Are you hurt?"

Heather shook her head against his hand. "How did you know I was here?"

"Let's just say your friends were worried about you." He tipped his head.

Heather narrowed her gaze, confusion making her thinking fuzzy. "Thank God." She raised her eyebrows. "Oh, my. I have to make sure Maryann and Ruthie are okay."

Zach brushed a soft kiss across her forehead and she smiled up at him. "They are. They called the sheriff's department. Deputy Gates is on his way. He can take care of Fiona."

"I'm not going anywhere." Fiona tried to get

her feet under her, but she couldn't seem to with her hands handcuffed behind her back.

Zach grabbed Fiona's arm and yanked her to her feet.

Heather shook her head. "She had befriended Brian. She wanted to write his story." She turned and glared at Fiona.

Heather took a big step back when Fiona puckered her lips as if to spit on her.

Heather blinked slowly, trying to tamp down her growing anger. She was done being the victim. She spun around and walked out onto the porch. She'd fill Zach in with all the details soon. But right now, she needed to find her friends. The cool air felt refreshing on her warm cheeks. Out of the corner of her eye, she saw movement.

She turned and saw Maryann and Ruthie running toward her, their long dresses flapping around their legs.

Heather ran down the stairs and pulled Ruthie into an embrace. Then she quickly let her Amish friend go. "Thank you for calling the sheriff."

"I've never been more grateful we had a phone in the barn for business purposes." Maryann reached out and squeezed Heather's hand.

A commotion drew their attention to the

front porch. Zach led Fiona out in handcuffs to the newly arrived sheriff's deputy.

"Are you okay, Maryann?" Heather asked.

"*Yah*. I'm fine."

"I'm sorry you got wrapped up in this."

"I've had enough excitement around here to last me a lifetime, that's for sure." Maryann shook her bonneted head. "Everything's okay now."

Zach joined them after Fiona was secured in the back of the patrol car. "Is everyone okay? Does anyone need medical attention?"

"*Neh*," Maryann said. "I'm fine."

"Is she going to jail?" Ruthie asked.

"Yes. Then she'll await trial," Zach said.

"But she won't get out to hurt us?" Ruthie asked.

"No, she won't."

"I need to go inside. Sit down." Maryann walked toward the steps.

Ruthie turned to follow her in and Heather called out to her, "I'll be in in a minute to help you clean up." She didn't think there was too much damage, but some furniture and items had been upended when she and Fiona had struggled. And the glass from the pitcher would need to be swept up.

Heather felt slightly awkward as she and Zach stood in silence watching the patrol car pull away. Deputy Gates said Heather could come in later to file a report.

"Ruthie and Maryann have become like family to you."

Heather rubbed her upper arms for warmth. "They have. I'm so grateful they're okay." She stared at the empty road. "If only Brian could have put his charms to work for something positive." Heather sniffed and drew her shoulders up.

"You're going to have to relay the entire story of what happened here to the sheriff's department," Zach said, placing his hand on the small of her back.

"I'd be happy to never hear Brian Fox's name again."

"Me, too. He's caused a lot of havoc in our lives."

Heather lifted her hand toward the house. "Well, I better go help them clean up." With her heart beating in her throat, she took a few steps toward the house, then turned to call Zach's name when he said hers at the same time.

"You go first," Zach said, smiling.

Heather cleared her throat and she grew light-headed. "Okay, I'm just going to say this because about thirty minutes ago I thought I had bought the farm. Well, I had bought the farm, but...you know what I mean."

Zach nodded, a light glowing in his eyes. He seemed to be enjoying this. "Go on..." he encouraged her.

"Anyway...I should know that life and a future are not guaranteed for anyone. And—" she lifted a shoulder, feeling so far out of her element she wanted to run into the cornfields and hide "—is this thing between us going to lead anywhere?"

Heather was standing in front of him pouring her heart out. All of a sudden, her face flushed red and she threw up her hands. "Just... I don't know. Forget it. I need to go help them clean up." She spun around.

Zach reached out and touched her arm. "Heather. Wait."

She stopped with her back to him and paused a minute before turning around. When she did, she had tears in her eyes. Without saying anything, he stepped toward her and pulled her into an embrace. He ran his hand over her head, feeling her silky smooth hair and breathing in the fresh scent of her cucumber shampoo.

"I've faced a lot of bad guys in my career. Been put in a ton of hairy situations. But I have never been more frightened than when I found out you were in danger today." He pulled away slightly and cupped her face in his hands and pressed his lips against hers. After a long moment, he pulled away. "I don't know what I would have done if I had lost you."

Heather smiled and a tear trailed down her cheek.

"I should have never let you out of my sight," Zach said.

She swallowed hard. "You have your job in Buffalo. I have the bed-and-breakfast here in Quail Hollow."

"Those are jobs. You're more important to me than a job."

A small line creased her forehead, indecision flashing in her eyes. "But I've worked so hard on the bed-and-breakfast. I wanted to honor my family."

A small pool of dread gathered in his stomach. Didn't she feel the same way? He dropped his hands and stepped away. He needed her to understand exactly how he felt, then he'd walk away if that was what she really wanted.

He met her gaze. "I think I'm falling in love with you, Heather."

She reached out and took his hand in hers. "You're such a sweet man. But I can't give up everything here for you. I know you're nothing like Brian, but I need to be independent. Not cave to the wishes of a boyfriend."

Zach tried to process everything that she was

saying to him while not showing the disappointment on his face. "I wouldn't ask you to leave Quail Hollow. We can work something out. Buffalo's not that far. I could commute. Or find a new job. They need law enforcement here, too."

It was Heather's turn to touch his cheek. "I care for you a lot, Zach. But my heart needs to heal. I've been through so much that I don't trust myself."

"I understand. And I'll wait for you."

EPILOGUE

A year later...

Heather handed Ruthie the last dish. Her Amish friend dried it and put it away in the cabinet. The Quail Hollow Bed & Breakfast was booked solid this weekend. The fall foliage was at its peak, the sun was shining and a big event was happening in their very backyard. The tourists who'd happened to book this weekend were in for a very big treat.

"I don't know why I'm so nervous," Heather said, drying her hand on a dish towel.

"No need. The members of the Amish community are experts at barn raising."

Heather touched her hair, trying to remember if she had even combed it this morning. "Do you think we have enough food?"

"Of course. And don't forget many of the wives will be coming with picnic baskets, too."

Heather let out a long breath. Through the

kitchen window, she noticed her neighbors starting to arrive and strolling over to the foundation that had been set last week in preparation for the walls and roof. "I suppose we should get out there."

Ruthie smiled and held out her hand as if to say, *After you.*

Heather stepped outside in her jeans and T-shirt, surprisingly not needing a sweater in October.

Ruthie came up beside her. "Um, you realize you can't help rebuild the barn, right? The men do the work."

A row of buggies were lined up along the property. The men had unhitched the horses and let them graze in the fenced-off area. Heather couldn't wait to have her own horse there.

"Oh, I know. I'm afraid of heights anyway."

"Do you think they'll let *me* help?" Zach strode through the gathering crowd of Amish workmen on the lawn and stuffed a broad-brimmed hat on his head. "Like my hat? Sloppy Sam let me borrow it."

Heather couldn't help but smile. "You made it!" She and Zach had been carrying on a long-distance relationship for the past year with Zach coming to visit Quail Hollow when he could. And Heather visiting Buffalo during the quiet season. They had also spent some time together during the subsequent trials. The woman who had helped Brian escape from prison was serving a minimum of seven years in prison. Fiona had received a much harsher sentence for killing Brian and kidnapping Heather, Maryann and Ruthie. Fiona would never likely see the light of day again. Heather was satisfied that the impressionable young woman wouldn't be bothering her anymore, but she couldn't help but feel sad that Brian Fox had destroyed yet another life.

"I wouldn't miss this barn raising for the world," Zach said. "The Amish could teach us a thing or two about getting things done." He took a few steps and studied the construction zone. "I see they already laid the foundation." He turned around and smiled at Heather, a smile that melted her heart. "A strong foundation is key."

Heather crossed her arms as a warm tingle raced down her spine. "A strong foundation *is* very important."

"Hey, I thought you wanted to help," Sloppy Sam hollered as he pulled a ladder from the back of his wagon.

Zach tipped his hat. "Duty calls."

Heather smiled and watched Zach jog over to offer a hand.

Ruthie leaned over and whispered into Heather's ear. "He looks very handsome."

"You're never going to stop, are you?"

Ruthie playfully tugged on the strings of her bonnet. "*Neh*. Everyone needs their happily-ever-after."

Zach put in a full day's work unlike any he had ever had. Despite being active and physically fit, every single muscle in his body ached. All the Amish neighbors had left for the day, with a handful promising to return tomorrow for some finishing touches.

Zach stepped back and admired the structure that had gone up quickly by the well-timed work of the Amish. He considered himself blessed to have experienced such teamwork. Such community. It was heartwarming.

Running the back of his hand across his forehead, he let out a long breath. The sky behind the barn—a barn that hadn't existed just twelve hours ago—was gorgeous, a mix of deep purple, orange and red.

"It's beautiful, isn't it?"

Zach turned around to find Heather walking across the lawn, dressed in jeans, a T-shirt and a light jacket. Her long brown hair was twirled into a loose bun. "Yes, beautiful." But he wasn't referring to the barn or the sky behind it.

A light twinkled in her eyes and she tipped her head shyly. "I can't believe how quickly it went up. I love it."

"The community has really embraced you."

Heather pressed her hands to her chest. "I'm blessed." A hint of nostalgia tinged her tone. "I feel like the new barn is like a rebirth. No longer a reminder of the tragedy that was, but rather hope for the future." She dragged a finger across her lower lip. "I think I've made peace with my mother's death, despite the unanswered questions. I've found forgiveness and I know the man who took her from us will be judged in the end."

She drew in a deep breath and smiled despite watery eyes. "Come spring, I'll house my own horse in the barn. I'd love to ride."

"Sounds like a great plan." Watching her intently, Zach took off his hat and tossed it on the grass. "I also have plans for the spring."

"Oh?"

Zach had a hard time reading her expression. Dread? Excitement? Anticipation?

He slid his fingers into his back pocket and eased out a diamond ring. He must have touched it a million times during the workday, assuring himself it was still there. Assuring himself that Heather also felt the same way about him.

Her gaze dropped to the ring pinched between his fingers. Her eyes flared bright. He dropped to one knee. "Miss Heather Miller, will you marry me?"

The ground under Heather's feet shifted as Zach's words took a minute to hit their intended mark.

Will you marry me?

Zach watched her, anticipation etched on his handsome features.

"But your job in Buffalo…" She turned around and flung her hand awkwardly toward the bed-and-breakfast, completely refinished, as if to say, *And my work.*

The new barn… Her plans for a horse.

Her mind swirled…

"We can work around that. A job is a job. But I can't live my life without you. That I know for sure. I've missed you over this past year. I don't want to do long distance anymore."

Hope, excitement and love blossomed in her heart.

Heather leaned over and cupped his cheeks in her hands, drawing him to his feet and pulling him into an embrace. She loved the feel of his solid chest, his firm grip, his warm lips on hers.

He pulled back and looked at her, a question in his kind eyes. "You never answered me."

"Yes, *yes*, I'll marry you." Butterflies flitted in her stomach and she could feel the joy radiating from her soul.

He stepped back and took her hand and slid the ring on her finger.

"I love you, Heather."

"I love you, too."

Zach lifted her hand to his lips and kissed her fingers.

"So, you finally did it."

Heather spun around at the sound of Ruthie's voice.

"You knew?" Heather asked.

"It was simply a matter of time. I think everyone knew you two were destined for each other, except you."

Heather took a step back and Zach hugged her from behind. She tilted her head back to rest on his solid chest. He ran his knuckles gently up and down her arm.

"I'm thrilled for you guys. But does this mean I'm out of a job? I heard Marshal Walker's a great cook," Ruthie joked.

"He *is* a great cook, but you've got official bed-and-breakfast duty."

"Sounds perfect," Zach said.

Heather looked up at Zach and he kissed her on the nose. "It *is* perfect," Heather said.

"The kitchen's all cleaned up. Sloppy Sam's

going to give me a ride home." Ruthie took a step backward.

"Oh, really?" Heather said playfully.

"Knock it off," Ruthie said. "I think we've had enough lovey-dovey stuff for a while."

"You never know," Heather said. "You never know."

Ruthie waved her hand in dismissal. Heather thought she heard her giggling as she strolled away and hopped up into Sam's wagon.

Zach threaded his fingers with hers. "I should probably call my father and share the good news. He was convinced you'd find yourself a nice Amish guy if I didn't make my move soon."

Heather leaned over and grabbed the broad-brimmed hat from the grass and stuffed it on Zach's head. She leaned up on her tippy-toes and planted a kiss on his lips. "As much as I love you, you'd never pass for Amish."

* * * * *

Dear Reader,

I hope you enjoyed *Plain Sanctuary*. This book was my sixth Amish story written for Love Inspired Suspense, but my first set in the new fictional town of Quail Hollow, New York. I decided the sleepy Amish town of Apple Creek needed a little break from the murder and mayhem. I wanted my characters there to enjoy their happily-ever-afters—for a little while. But I'm sure the characters living there will start whispering in my ear, forcing me to eventually tell their stories.

I love receiving reader letters telling me how much you've enjoyed my stories and how you want to hear more about a certain character. I'm thrilled when I can respond that that character's story is already in the next book! I also have hopes of writing more stories set in Quail Hollow, too. The reader desire for Amish stories appears strong, and as long as that's true, I'll be plotting a way to be a part of it. Thank you for loving these stories.

During my research, I've learned that New York State has a growing Amish population. The Amish have left other settlements in Ohio, Pennsylvania and other states to come to New York for a number of reasons, including seeking farmland, disagreeing with previous settlements over rules, or perhaps because they're trying to escape state laws that would impact their daily life. Because of this, I felt comfortable creating Quail Hollow as a not-too-distant settlement from Apple Creek, which is loosely based on one of the oldest settlements of Amish in Western New York. I've also received many letters from readers who currently live (or previously lived) in Western New York and they love the Buffalo-area connection. I hope you do, too, even if you're not from the area. It's a beautiful part of the country.

As always, I love to hear from my readers. If you'd like to stay abreast of all my releases, please go to my website, www.AlisonStone.com, and sign up for my digital newsletter. Feel free to email me at Alison@AlisonStone.com or mail a letter to me at PO Box 333, Buffalo, NY 14051.

Sincerely,

Alison Stone

Get 2 Free Books,
Plus 2 Free Gifts—
just for trying the
Reader Service!

Get 2 Free Books,
Plus 2 Free Gifts—
just for trying the Reader Service!

HARLEQUIN
HEARTWARMING

HOMETOWN HEARTS ♥

YES! Please send me **The Hometown Hearts Collection** in Larger Print. This collection begins with 3 FREE books and 2 FREE gifts in the first shipment. Along with my 3 free books, I'll also get the next 4 books from the Hometown Hearts Collection, in LARGER PRINT, which I may either return and owe nothing, or keep for the low price of $4.99 U.S./ $5.89 CDN each plus $2.99 for shipping and handling per shipment*. If I decide to continue, about once a month for 8 months I will get 6 or 7 more books, but will only need to pay for 4. That means 2 or 3 books in every shipment will be FREE! If I decide to keep the entire collection, I'll have paid for only 32 books because 19 books are FREE! I understand that accepting the 3 free books and gifts places me under no obligation to buy anything. I can always return a shipment and cancel at any time. My free books and gifts are mine to keep no matter what I decide.

262 HCN 3432 462 HCN 3432

Name	(PLEASE PRINT)	
Address		Apt. #
City	State/Prov.	Zip/Postal Code

Signature (if under 18, a parent or guardian must sign)

Mail to the **Reader Service**:

IN U.S.A.: P.O. Box 1867, Buffalo, NY. 14240-1867
IN CANADA: P.O. Box 609, Fort Erie, Ontario L2A 5X3

* Terms and prices subject to change without notice. Prices do not include applicable taxes. Sales tax applicable in NY. Canadian residents will be charged applicable taxes. This offer is limited to one order per household. All orders subject to approval. Credit or debit balances in a customer's account(s) may be offset by any other outstanding balance owed by or to the customer. Please allow 4 to 6 weeks for delivery. Offer available while quantities last. Offer not available to Quebec residents.

Your Privacy—The Reader Service is committed to protecting your privacy. Our Privacy Policy is available online at www.ReaderService.com or upon request from the Reader Service.

We make a portion of our mailing list available to reputable third parties that offer products we believe may interest you. If you prefer that we not exchange your name with third parties, or if you wish to clarify or modify your communication preferences, please visit us at www.ReaderService.com/consumerchoice or write to us at Reader Service Preference Service, P.O. Box 9062, Buffalo, NY. 14240-9062. Include your complete name and address.

HHBPA17

READERSERVICE.COM

Manage your account online!

- Review your order history
- Manage your payments
- Update your address

*We've designed the
Reader Service website
just for you.*

Enjoy all the features!

- Discover new series available to you, and read excerpts from any series.
- Respond to mailings and special monthly offers.
- Browse the Bonus Bucks catalog and online-only exculsives.
- Share your feedback.

Visit us at:
ReaderService.com